Goodbye Old Paint

R. L. Blackledge

Copyright © 2012 R. L. Blackledge
All rights reserved.

ISBN: 1-4609-7286-4
ISBN-13: 9781460972861

"White Shepherd in the Mountains" image copyright
AnetaPics/shutterstock.com

To my mother,
who struggled through the Great Depression
with courage and love

Chapter One   February

Everyone knew in those days of the Great Depression that thirteen was an unlucky number. And thinking back to that time, more than 75 years ago, I remember having plenty of bad luck after I turned twelve and began my thirteenth year. But I had some good luck, too. For one thing, that was when old Paint came into my life and, before the year was over, he saved me once from near disaster and twice from almost certain death.

The big white mongrel dog appeared out of nowhere one cold February afternoon in that small Wyoming town where I lived with my mother, older brother, and younger sister. I was scuffing along an alley, part of my usual route to and from school, kicking at rocks and looking for cardboard boxes I could trade to Stein's Bakery for day-old doughnuts and sweet rolls.

I planned to do my chores at home and then take my ice skates to the river. There I skated and hunted with my pal Kenneth during the cold months and fished and swam in the warm season.

I kicked another rock from the ice and watched it skitter swiftly far down the alley. Then I saw the dog, one I'd never seen before. It came padding along toward me, wary, but alert and proud as though it knew it wasn't any ordinary dog. It was almighty skinny and, I felt sure, had no regular source of food or shelter.

The dog looked like a cross between a big hound and a German shepherd. His bone-white fur was dirty. On his gaunt left flank was a plate-size splotch of dried green paint. A few paces away, he stopped and examined me. Then he grinned and wagged his tail as a dog will do when he knows he's met a friend. I stretched out a hand and called, "Here, boy. Come on." He hesitated, whined, and then approached and began licking my outstretched fingers. I hugged him around the neck and buried my face in the wet dog-smell of his fur.

Then I stood up and pondered the next move. I wanted to keep him. I had wanted a dog *forever*. But with money so scarce in those hard times, a brother and sister at home, and a baby on the way, I knew my mother would be in no mood to take on another mouth to feed. Mother was strong-willed but also as soft-hearted as they come. If I could only persuade her to let me keep the dog while I looked for its owner, she'd probably want to keep him, too. And whoever had daubed the dog with paint and turned him out to starve wouldn't likely want him back.

Paint. A good name, I thought. I began backing down the alley while the dog sat watching me. I snapped my fingers and whistled and called, "Come on, Paint. Let's go. Attaboy, Paint." He got to his feet and began following me. I turned and skipped and ran down the alley toward our house with my new dog bounding alongside me.

The alley ran into Crane Street then continued on. Before crossing I looked both ways from force of habit. Roaring up the street toward me in a cloud of dust was Dwayne Tyler's Model A Ford.

I was mortally afraid of Dwayne because he was cruel and treacherous and especially enjoyed picking on me. I ran as fast as I could whenever he came in sight. He enjoyed nothing more than to catch me and impose whatever indignity and pain he fancied at the moment.

Dwayne's favorite trick, before I learned to avoid him, was to grasp the back of my neck and walk along beside me, chatting and ever so friendly. Then he'd kick my rear foot sideways so I'd stumble and fall face down on the sidewalk. He'd stand over me and bray his mean laugh.

"Whatsa matter," he'd taunt. "Ain't the little baby learned to walk yet? Here. Get up and I'll teach ya."

He'd haul me to my feet and start off beside me and then do it again and again, until I'd manage to get away. Then he'd stand laughing fit to kill until I was out of earshot.

Dwayne was a year out of high school, big and muscular, and, some said, quite handsome. He never had a job but always had money. I heard a neighbor lady tell my mother that Dwayne's spinster aunt, whom he lived with, had scads of money and she'd spoiled the boy rotten. My mother had replied no one could spoil such a bad egg. Older girls and young women around town liked him. One or another could be seen most every evening riding around in his car and later going up to park on the bluff overlooking the river.

The summer before, when my friend Kenneth and I were just learning to swim, Dwayne's favorite sport was to catch us near the river and throw us in, clothes and all. He thought it great fun to watch us floundering and gasping in the water. He'd kick us to prevent our getting back onto the bank until we paddled down the current way below him and crawled out mighty nigh drowned.

That same summer Dwayne built, out behind his Aunt's barn, a fabulous castle of big cardboard boxes, with towers of smaller boxes glued onto the corners. He painted doors and windows on it. Kenneth and I observed his work from a safe distance, ignoring invitations to go inside the castle. One day we saw him put a cat inside the cardboard structure and then light a match to one corner. The flames spread quickly until it was all ablaze and looked like a real building on fire. A hole burned through one wall and the cat leaped out, its fur afire, yowling in agony. Dwayne struck the cat with a heavy stick and shoved it back into the flaming, collapsing castle. The look on his face was terrible to see, something between pleasure and hate. He watched until the cat's pitiful cries stopped and the burning cardboard castle lay in black ashes blowing in the breeze. I had nightmares about that for months, dreaming I was in the castle instead of the cat.

So that was what Dwayne was like. Beneath his good looks lurked a vicious kid who enjoyed destroying things and hurting people and animals. I feared he might see me, so I ducked quickly back into the alley and hid behind a shed until I saw his car zoom past. Then I ran across the street into the alley on the other side with my new dog grinning and cavorting beside me.

Upon reaching home, I led old Paint around to the back, hoping my mother hadn't seen me and the dog. I opened the door of the shed near the alley and urged Paint inside. He was more than a little apprehensive, but I coaxed him to lie down, kneeled and stroked his head.

"Now don't you worry, boy," I cajoled. "You stay here for just a few minutes and everything's gonna be fine. You'll see."

I shut the door and heard him whine and scratch at the wood. Then I hustled to our back door and entered the kitchen. I felt the warm air and smelled something good cooking. My mother was singing in her soft sweet voice as she poured a can of tomatoes into a big pot on the stove. The marvelous perfume of baking bread came from the oven.

It seemed to me that whenever I came home my mother was always singing—mostly church hymns—although sometimes I wondered what she had to sing about. When I thought on it at all, I knew her life was an endless round of work and struggling to make a little bit of money go a long ways. She didn't get to go skating or swimming at the river, or build snow forts, or hunt bird eggs, or do any of the things that filled my life with joy. Then I would resolve to do more of the work. But I soon forgot again.

She turned and smiled. "'Home is the hunter...home from the hill'," she teased. "Or is it Robin Hood? Or Sir Launcelot?"

"Oh, *Mom,*" I protested.

"How was school today?"

"School was awful. But after school...wait'll you hear what I found."

She sat on a chair. "I can't wait," she said. "It must be something wonderful."

"Oh, it *is,*" I said, only a wee shadow clouding my optimism. "You'll never guess. It's what I've always wanted."

"I'm glad. Everyone should have what he's always wanted...sometime. What *can* this marvel be?"

"It's a *dog,* Mom! It's the keenest dog ever. You're gonna love him."

Her smile faded. "Johnny, you can't just pick up any dog that comes along. If it's as fine a dog as you say, its owner will be looking for it."

"Oh, he hasn't got an owner. He's been turned out to starve."

"Well, supposing that is true, there are other problems."

"Which ones?"

"Like how are we going to feed him? You know what a struggle I have buying food for us. And the rent is due. And..."

"Oh, there's always a few scraps we don't eat. But, Mom, he's terrible hungry right now. Can't I give him <u>something</u>?"

She hesitated and tried to look stern. Then she sighed and her eyes softened. "Well, there's some oatmeal from breakfast. And those doughnuts you brought home. They're yours to give."

"No, Mom, they're ours. All for one and one for all. Like in the book you read me. Remember?"

"But Johnny, a dog needs meat. And the only meat we have is in the soup." She pointed to the stove.

"There'll be the bone," I argued. "We don't eat bones. But dogs love 'em. And Dr. Hammond still has part of a deer hanging in his barn. I bet he'll give me some bones with a little meat on 'em. And I have three gunny sacks. They're worth two cents each. I bet I could buy some meat for six cents."

She stood up and patted my head. "I don't know," she said sadly. "But I tell you what. We'll see how it goes until you find the dog's owner. You *will* try, won't you?"

"Sure, Mom. I'll try awful hard. Now let's go out and see him. You're just gonna love him, Mom."

She followed me out to the shed. I opened the door and Paint sat up. Right away he grinned and started thumping his big old tail on the floor. I could see my mother was surprised.

"That's a mighty big dog," she said. "I had in mind a small one like Mrs. Bailey's."

"Oh, *that* little mutt," I said. "Why he's hardly big enough for fish bait. Now, you take old Paint. He's strong enough to keep burglars away and all kinds of stuff. And Paint don't take up much room. He's ever so well behaved. He'd just hunker down behind the kitchen stove and you'd never even know he's there."

"Well," she said, "we don't have anything to attract burglars. And a little oatmeal won't fill him up. But bring him in and we'll see."

She started back on the packed snowpath to the house. I felt like it was opening day of the fishing season, Fourth of July, and Christmas all rolled into one.

I gave my dog a big hug and yelled, "Yippee! Paint, you got yourself the best home a dog ever had." I ran for the back door with the big white dog at my heels.

Our house was very small, rented to us by Old Lady Bailey, who lived down the street in a large, two-story, stone edifice. I thought she must be very rich because she had a fur coat and was always driving away in her car, all dressed up, and never seemed to work. Before the Great Depression began in 1930, I think we must have been rich, too. Then we lived in a big white house with lots of rooms and my father owned two cars.

When his refrigeration and radio business went broke, he found a job trying to sell cars. But during all the past winter he hadn't sold one. Buyers were scarcer than palm trees in Wyoming. Folks were lucky if they could pay rent and buy food. So my father took another job, trying to sell electric light plants to ranchers who didn't have any money either. The job was in South Dakota so he was away from home most of the time. He wasn't selling much but was sending us what money he could. My mother tried to find work but there simply weren't any jobs around, especially for women. So we moved from the big white house into the dinky, rundown place we now called home.

But that little house on a graveled street had everything a boy could want: my family and all outdoors to play in. The river flowed east from the nearby mountains to the edge of our town. Then it bent north a mile and then south again, outlining a tongue of land with the town in the middle. Along most of the river banks grew a jungle of cottonwood, willow, and boxelder trees where a boy could have endless adventures. Our house was about in the middle of the land tongue and so the river was near in three directions.

On an open porch fronting the house a wood-slat bench swing hung from two chains. Inside, the small living room, as we called it, held a davenport couch, which made into a bed for my sister Anna. On the left was my mother's tiny bedroom, crammed with a bed, chest of drawers, and dressing table, survivors of more prosperous times. Behind the living room was a small dining area, one corner occupied by a coal-fired heater. The kitchen, on the left, had a decrepit coal-burning cook stove, a sink, and a table where we ate meals when my father was gone. From the dining area a door opened to a short hallway alongside a little bathroom. The passageway led to another small bedroom where my brother Ralph and I slept, argued, and sometimes fought. That part of the house was very cold in winter. But in summer it was grand. Two unscreened windows allowed convenient entrance and exit without using front or back doors.

Of course, I never found the dog's owner nor anyone who remembered ever seeing him around. Dr. Hammond said someone probably just dropped him off in town. He gave me a big sack of bones and the neck meat from his deer carcass. And as the days passed I began to believe old Paint was really my dog. Although it was mighty slim pickings for his food.

I could hardly wait for my pal Kenneth to get out of quarantine for scarlet fever. In only two more days they'd take the sign off his house and he could come out and see my new dog. I had visited Kenneth nearly every day since the city official had tacked up the sign which warned no one was to enter or leave until the time was up. I would whistle outside his bedroom window until he opened it. And we'd talk. He hadn't looked as though he had scarlet fever very bad. But his brother had been real sick. Kenneth said he'd almost died.

The day finally came when Kenneth returned to school. At recess I told him about Paint and he was as excited to see the dog as I was to show him off.

That school day seemed to stretch on forever and I got in trouble twice for not paying attention. It wasn't serious trouble, because next to my mother, Miss Ruth Owen was the prettiest, nicest lady I knew. She was 20 and had come to our school the previous autumn after completing a year at a teachers' college.

She was slender, with dark hair and blue eyes, with always the hint of a smile on her lips. When she bent over my desk to help with my arithmetic, I could smell a faint perfume, like a fresh spring day. She must have had at least five dresses, because she wore a different one, ironed and crisp, everyday, not like my teacher the year before who wore the same dress for five days and then her other one the next week. Miss Owen never scolded, yelled, or hit me like my other teachers had. And I was in love with her.

The crawling hands of the clock finally reached the best moment of all: end of the school day. The classroom quiet erupted into a noisy hubbub of shouts and laughter, books slamming shut, and feet rushing toward the door.

Miss Owen spoke over the din, "Behave, children. Don't forget your manners." I looked back. She was smiling at me.

Kenneth was waiting near the school's side door. We grinned at each other and took off whooping and running toward our secret hideout three blocks from school.

It was behind an old barn set back from the alley fifty feet or so. Weathered chicken coops extended to the alley from each corner of the barn, forming three walls to enclose a space once used for unloading hay, I supposed. But Dr. Hammond, an animal doctor, who owned the barn and the house beyond it, no longer kept horses. He used the area for storing stacks of lumber left over from his dead father's construction business. A row of lilac bushes along the alley had interlaced to enclose the fourth side of the area. Through one small space in the thicket we gained entrance to our hideout. The rear of the barn faced south and the low winter sun would reflect off the walls and melt the snow there when it still lay deep and cold everywhere else. It was warm whenever the sun shone, and little wind reached that sheltered area even on the worst days.

As soon as we slithered through the hole in the thicket that afternoon, we stretched out on a stack of planks and luxuriated in the warmth and privacy, hidden from the prying eyes and interfering ways of grownups. I thought I'd tell Kenneth how I found my dog. And then we'd go to my house and see him. But Kenneth had something more pressing on his mind.

Before I could utter a word, he said "That Miss Owen is just about the purtiest thing I ever saw."

I was startled and immediately defensive. "You shouldn't oughta say *that*, Kenneth."

"Why not?" he challenged, sitting up.

"Because you shouldn't say such things about someone *I* love. That's why!" I sat up, too.

"What do *you* know about love?" he scoffed.

"Well, lots. I just never told you. I been loving her for a long, long time."

"Not as long as me, I bet."

"Yes, I have too. Longer. Probably two or three weeks. Before you got the scarlet fever."

"Hah! For me it's been four, maybe five weeks."

We jumped to our feet and faced each other like a couple of those game cocks a neighbor kept. Put 'em in a pen together and bang! right away they start fighting.

"You never did any such thing," I said. "I loved her first and what's more she loves me."

"That ain't true."

"You sayin' I'm a liar?"

"Yes! And double liar!"

"You take that back!"

"I won't!"

"Then I'll make you," I shouted.

"Just you try and you'll be sorry."

For a moment we stood glaring at each other, then at the same time each of us struck the other. The blows brought us momentarily still and silent, then we began shoving and punching and grunting and crying out in pain. We grappled and went down in the cold slush and rolled and struggled until we could fight no more. We got shakily to our feet.

"Do you take it back?" I said.

"No! Do you?"

"Not on your life." I picked up a little stick and put it on my shoulder.

"There," I said. "If you think you can whip me, knock that chip off."

He did and we started punching each other again and again and then clinched and wrestled each other to the ground. I got a scissors hold on him with my legs. He busted loose and got me around the chest with his arms. We kept thrashing around in the slush, first one then the other gaining a momentary advantage.

"If you wanna quit, say uncle," I'd say.

"No. *You* say uncle," he'd gasp. And then we'd go at it again. Finally we stopped, chests heaving, too exhausted to go on fighting. We lay there getting back our breath.

"Johnny," Kenneth said, after a long silence, "I don't think I can whip you."

I said, "I don't think I can lick you either." We sat up and stared at each other, all the fight worn out of us.

"Well, what're we gonna do?" I asked.

"I don't know. We can't both of us love her."

I pondered that obvious fact and then I had an idea.

"Well, why not?" I exclaimed. "You take those knights of King Arthur. Sir Launcelot loved the queen and he was the king's best friend."

"Didn't the king fight him?"

"I don't think so."

"So what happened?"

"I don't know. I had to take the book back before I finished it. But that don't matter, Kenneth. We can both love Miss Owen...from afar...just like Sir Launcelot."

"What's from afar mean?"

"It means you just love her and protect her but you never kiss or get married or any of that stuff."

Kenneth thought about that and so did I. We thought for quite a while.

Then he said, "Say, that's keen. But don't you have to swear or something to do that?"

"Of course," I said. "You have to take a solemn oath with somebody tapping you on the head with a sword. And we'll *do* it!"

And so we did. We took our swords, made of wooden laths, from their hiding place behind the stack of lumber. Kenneth knelt before me and I gave him the oath first so's he would know how.

"Do you, Sir Morgan, solemnly swear you will always love Maid Owen from afar? And never let her get into any danger but what you help her? And hope to die if you don't?"

Kenneth nodded and I touched him on the head with my sword.

"Golly," he said. "Sir Morgan. That's a keen name. Who're you gonna be?"

"I'll be Sir Benneville."

"Was he one of King Arthur's knights?"

"I don't know. Probably. But it's sure enough a grand name."

I knelt before Kenneth and he gave me the oath. I arose feeling very solemn and dedicated. We put the swords back in their hiding place. We were friends again.

"Hey, Kenneth," I said. "I almost forgot. You gotta come over and see my new dog."

We squeezed through the hole in the thicket and went running off toward my house.

From that first day I could see Kenneth loved old Paint as much as I did. And the dog liked Kenneth, too, almost as much as me. Maybe *just* as much. And after school and on weekends the three of us had great times. We'd take Paint down to the river and he would chase us, sliding and slithering on the ice, while he tried to catch us as we sprinted and dodged around on our skates. Or one of us would grab his tail and he'd pull us, his claws digging into the ice. He was a strong dog.

Then the month was nearly half over. A February thaw began to melt the snow, and patches of dirt and winter-brown grass came into view again. Ice began melting from the streets and water ran in little rivers in the gutters and down the alleys and collected in small ponds in the low places. Going home from school I would put little sticks in the flowing water and imagine they were canoes filled with painted Indians pursuing another canoe of bearded trappers, the canoes racing down the torrents running through canyons in the melting ice. It was fun to wade and splash in the ponds. My mother would scold me when I got home, my boots wet and water splashed on my jeans. She wouldn't let me go out again until my boots had dried near the kitchen stove.

Shortly before Valentine's Day, Kenneth and I decided we'd give Miss Owen something very special as a token of our vows to love her from afar. We shopped several stores, thinking to get her a red heart-shaped box of chocolates. But the smallest ones cost 50 cents, and the bigger ones cost a dollar or even more. We were astounded and discouraged to learn how expensive love could be.

Then at the dime store we spotted some little red heart-shaped boxes priced two for a nickel. We decided we would fill one with a penny's worth of little candy hearts with sentiments printed on them—like "Be Mine" and "Love" and mushy stuff like that. All that remained was how to pay for such a fabulous valentine.

"Two cents is all I have," Kenneth said.

"I got six cents from selling my gunny sacks," I said. "I was gonna buy some meat for Paint, but I'll try to get some more deer bones from Dr. Hammond."

I thought about the large difference in our wealth.

"I tell you what," I said. "I'll buy two boxes and you buy two cents worth of the candy hearts."

"What're we gonna do with two boxes?" Kenneth wondered.

"We'll put half the candy in Miss Owen's box and half in the other one and I'll give *it* to my mother."

"What about *my* mother?"

"I'm putting up a nickel for the boxes and you're only spending two cents for the candy. Fair is fair, isn't it?"

Kenneth was silent for a while then reluctantly he agreed.

"I'll give my mother the valentine I made in school," he said. "She doesn't care much for candy anyway."

"Now, we gotta sign a little piece of paper and put it in the box," I said. "But we won't use our real names. We'll sign it from Sir Benneville and Sir Morgan."

"Why not the other way around?"

"Well, they always do it that way—like in Miss Owen's roster. The Bs come before the Ms."

I could see he was not pleased, so I said, "That's okay, Kenneth. We don't have to do like everyone else. We'll sign it the other way 'round if you want to."

The next day was one of those too few occasions scattered throughout the school year when the task of learning was brightened briefly by a celebration. Like May Day. And in the fall came Halloween, then Thanksgiving, then the Christmas party. And now Valentine's Day.

Miss Owen had covered a cardboard box with white paper and pasted some red hearts on it. A slit in the box top received the valentines students gave one another. Near the end of the day Miss Owen opened the box after quite a long talk about why people give valentines. Some of the girls gave a valentine to everyone in class. I got two of those, including one from Gwendolyn Chesley. Beneath the verse she'd printed "I like you best of all, Gwendolyn C." I hated her about equally with all other girls my age, but for a moment I wavered because of what she'd written on the card. I crammed her valentine into my rear pocket so's no one would see it. Another one, unsigned, said: "You're a mellow fellow—And shaped just like a cello." I hadn't put a single valentine in the box. Nearly all my wealth had gone for the two heart-shaped boxes.

I received one that brought a flush to my cheeks. It was signed, "Fondly, Miss Owen." She *knows*, I thought. Bobby Smith turned around in his seat and showed me his valentine from Miss Owen. It was signed the same way. Gwendolyn tripped over to my desk and showed me another. Signed the same.

"Show me *your* valentines," she giggled. "I bet you got a very special one from a girl in this class."

I dug her crumpled little card from my pocket and mumbled, "I was gonna show it to my mother."

"It's really true what it says, Johnny." She giggled again and fled back to her seat.

Miss Owen brought out another box. In it were tiny paper cups with a few red heart candies in each. She gave one to each of us and then dismissed the class with a loving smile.

Outside Kenneth awaited my plodding arrival.

"Look what I got," he said, and showed me another valentine signed "Fondly, Miss Owen."

"Yeah, so did Bobby and Gwendolyn. I got one, too. I s'pose everybody did. Signed exactly like that."

His face showed his disappointment.

"But, you know, Kenneth," I said, "I've just figured it out. She *had* to do it that way…to cover her tracks. But it's only us she really loves."

"I bet you're right," he said.

At home I hurried through my chores: chopped an armload of kindling and hauled it and two buckets of coal into the kitchen and carried out the ashes from the stoves. I told my mother I was going over to Kenneth's for a while. Then I scooted away on my bike, old Paint loping along beside me.

My bicycle wasn't much. I'd found the rusty frame, cracked seat and rear wheel one day in an alley among a pile of junk discarded when someone had moved away. It took me a year to find and swap other valuables for the handle bars and a front wheel. The bike was rickety and both wheels wobbled. It had no fenders, so when the streets were wet I acquired a streak of mud spatters up the front and back of my clothes and on my face. But it was better than no bike at all.

Our plan was to deliver Miss Owen's valentine just before dark at the back door of the house where she rented the upstairs rooms. We had to avoid being seen. After all, how could you love from afar if you just walked up to the front door and handed her a box of candy? The house was on the edge of town. Behind all the houses on her street was a large fenced pasture. To reach her back door without being seen we must ride our bikes about a mile and then walk through the field.

So, late that afternoon we pedaled around the back road, parked our bikes, and, with Paint trotting beside us, started across the field. We noticed up in one corner, quite a way off, was the bull Old Man Schaeffer had brought up from Mexico. Dr. Hammond said it was a fighting bull and really shouldn't be kept so close to town. I figured that was why there weren't any cows or steers around. The bull started loping in our direction, so we ran to the barbed wire fence, scrambled under it and went on through the back yard of Miss Owen's house.

We rapped on the door and after a bit old Mrs. Jones peered out, obviously startled and suspicious to see two boys and a dog. We handed her the little box with "Miss Owen" printed on it and ran back and squeezed under the fence.

It was dusk when, about halfway back to the other fence, we spied the bull trotting toward us from the far corner of the pasture. We walked faster then toward the fence, not really scared, but not wanting to chance getting chased by the bull.

A few hundred feet from the fence I heard an ominous snort and looking back saw the bull was close behind us. Kenneth and I froze for a moment, wondering what to do. The bull stopped, pawed at the ground, tossed his head, then lowered it, aiming those two sharp horns straight at us. That made up our minds. We began edging away when suddenly he started for us. Kenneth darted off at one angle and I took another, running as fast as I could. I had on a light gray sweatshirt and I guess the bull favored that because he came after me, grunting and trotting with his head lowered and those two horns coming right at me. Just then I tripped and fell to the ground. I closed my eyes tight and pulled my knees up to my chest to make the smallest possible target. I thought my time had surely come.

But instead of feeling those sharp horns piercing my body I heard a loud bellow and a dog's fierce growling. I opened my eyes and saw Paint snapping at the bull's hind legs. The bull stopped and swung his head around suddenly and knocked old Paint sprawling. Then the bull made as if to spear Paint with his horns. I scrambled up, ran back and kicked the bull hard on its flank. He roared again and whirled around. Paint leaped to his feet. I sprinted for the fence with the bull in pursuit. I rolled under the bottom wire and crawled quickly away on hands and knees, wanting to get as far away as possible, terrified that the bull would charge right through the fence.

I looked back and saw Paint running and dodging beside the bull, and then the dog sprang and bit the bull on its nose. That brought forth the loudest bellow of all. And then Paint turned, streaked toward me, and crawled under the fence. The bull crashed smack into one of the thick new fence posts on which Old Man Shaeffer had strung strong new barbed wire. I feared the animal would come right through after me. The post cracked but the new wire didn't break. The bull stood head down, seeming dazed from the shock of striking the post. Then it gave a mournful bellow, as if wondering what in tarnation had happened to him.

Kenneth came running down the fence line to where I'd crossed. We were both breathing hard, our chests heaving from the exertion and the fear.

"Are you okay?" he asked, watching me brush the dirt from my clothes.

"Yeah. Thanks to our dog. Did ya see him take after that bull?"

"I saw you go back and kick him when he was about to stick his horns into Paint. I though you were both goners."

Old Paint was running back and forth on our side of the fence, barking at the bull, teasing him, but careful not to cross under the fence.

"Here, Paint," I called. "Let him alone. We don't want him to try that fence again."

Paint came to me and stood grinning and wagging his big tail, as if to say he'd never had so much fun before.

Kenneth and I walked over to the road where we'd left our bikes in the barrow pit, got on them and started pedaling home in the gathering darkness, glad to be unhurt and alive.

By the time I reached home I was late for dinner. And the rule was: if you were late, you had to do the dishes whether it was your turn or not. My sister was glad because it had been her turn.

After I'd eaten, I cleared the table and stood dabbling dreamily at dishes in the sink. My mother came up behind and hugged me.

"That was a beautiful valentine, Johnny. But where did you get the money?"

"I sold my gunny sacks, Mom. And you deserve it."

"Well, it's the loveliest valentine I ever had." She gave me another hug and left the kitchen. I wondered if Miss Owen felt that way about her valentine.

A few days later Kenneth and I noticed that Old Man Schaeffer had moved his bull from the pasture and turned his other cattle back in. This cleared the way for us to continue loving and serving Miss Owen from afar and make other trips across the pasture to make sure she wasn't in any danger we could save her from.

The next Saturday we rode down the street fronting Miss Owen's place, being careful not to look at the house. But we couldn't help seeing Dwayne Tyler's Model A Ford parked in front. It was a great shock, because we hated and feared Dwayne most of anyone in town. And so, when we saw his car parked at Miss Owen's house that day, Kenneth and I knew she was in for trouble.

After that we went by her house more often. We would ride past in daylight or, when Dwayne's car was there at night, park our bikes and approach the house in the shadows to see what was going on. The lights would be only in Mrs. Jones' downstairs rooms and through the windows we could see Dwayne and Miss Owen sitting in the parlor talking and laughing.

One night, when Mrs. Jones had gone out, Dwayne suddenly strode over to Miss Owen's chair and pulled her to her feet. Then he put his arms around her and kissed her for a long time. She struggled at first and then seemed to hug him back. But then she pushed him away. He said something and she replied. An angry look came over his face and then he turned and stalked from the room. She was crying. The front door slammed and we saw Dwayne throw open his car door and drive away very fast.

Kenneth laughed quietly and said, "Looks like she's one girl who ain't goin' to go and park on the bluff with Dwayne."

"Don't be so sure," I said. "You know *him*. He don't ever quit trying to get something he wants."

"That's right," Kenneth said solemnly. "We gotta watch out she don't get tangled up with that snake."

And for a week Dwayne's car wasn't parked in front of Miss Owen's house. Then he began visiting her again. We plotted ways to save her but came up with only the most foolish plans.

The last Saturday that month was a lucky one. Kenneth and I found four beer bottles and a pop bottle. We could get a penny apiece for them at Mrs. Redd's store. And to that establishment we hustled on our bikes, Paint ranging around before us, sniffing and raising a hind leg here and there.
"We'll have five cents," I said.
"Yeah. Two cents each and a penny left over."
"Maybe for a penny she'll give us some meat for Paint. Or if she won't, we'll buy three cents worth. And that leaves a penny apiece for candy."
"Okay," Kenneth said. "After all he helped us find the bottles."
Some people said Mrs. Redd was the town crazy. But she didn't seem so to us. She tolerated boys, which was more than you could say for most grownups. She had a little grocery store fronting some worthless land down near the railroad tracks. Behind the store were an old barn, a chicken coop with a wire fence around it but no chickens, and a ramshackle collection of a dozen small huts built of old boards from packing crates and shingled with strips of tin cut from cans. The shacks were bigger but not much better than dog houses. In them stayed a constantly changing population of down-on-their-luck bums and derelicts of every description. They were dirty, unshaven, but well behaved—as long as they were at Mrs. Redd's. She saw to that. She called them her "gentlemen lodgers." And some of them may have been "gentlemen" at some time or other. You never knew what a man had been through in those times.

The bell over Mrs. Redd's door tinkled loudly as we entered. Paint remained outside, peering through the door's window and whining. She came from behind the store's rear partition, red-painted lips smiling from a round but wrinkle-creased face beneath a high-piled mop of intensely red hair. As usual her clothing was entirely red, of various shades and condition from shabby to near-new.

She stopped behind the candy counter before which we stood eyeing her cornucopia of mouth watering sweets. Rows of chocolate candy bars in their boxes took half the glass-topped display case. But in the other half Mrs. Redd kept the biggest variety of penny candies in town: all colors of jaw breakers and suckers; red and black licorice ropes; small packets of powdered fruit flavors to mix with water; little wax bottles filled with colored sweet liquids; bubble gum; everything imaginable and each only a penny.

"You come sellin' or buyin'?" she asked.

"Well, both, Mrs. Redd," I said.

She took the bottles and laid five pennies on the counter.

"How much meat could we get for a penny?" I asked.

"Let's see. Hamburger's 15 cents a pound." She put a little dab on her scales. "That's about a penny's worth right there."

"That sure isn't much," Kenneth said. "How much for three cents?"

"That'd be one fifth of a pound. I'll make it a quarter pound because you boys is good customers." She placed a larger dab on the scales.

"Why, our dog would eat that in one bite," I said.

She looked outside and saw Paint, his nose pressed against the door glass.

"Well, whyn't you say so? I got some bones out back. Some meat on 'em. They don't smell so good. But dogs don't care about that. In fact, usually dogs *prefer* meat that's a little

Chapter Two   March

That year March came in like a pack of wolves, howling down from the north, snarling and slashing with icy teeth at the baby Spring. The blizzard raged all one night and into the next evening. When it wore itself out, snow drifts were high as the fences and below-zero cold moved in.

The storm brought worry to my mother, who'd kept an anxious eye on the coal shed, hoping she wouldn't have to buy more fuel for a while. Grownups, in general, hated the storm. They'd had enough of winter. But the big, new snowfall brought joy to boys like me. I always hoped for a snowstorm so bad they'd close the school. But no matter how deep the snow, we were expected to get to the schoolhouse and on time.

The morning after the storm my brother and I shoveled a path through the deep snow out to the coal shed. Then we cleared a path in front of the house, measuring carefully so neither did more than his half. I thought shoveling a path alongside the street was a dreadful waste. It was more fun to wade through the soft whiteness in my knee-high leather boots with jeans tucked in the tops to keep the snow out. But my mother always said, "We may be poor but we're not trash. Decent folks clear their sidewalks."

It was doggone cold, but I scarcely noticed. My old corduroy coat with sheepskin lining and collar and a sheepskin-lined, leather helmet fastened under my chin kept me warm as any Eskimo.

I started for school, wading through the deepest places, carefully avoiding where it had been shoveled. I didn't go through the alleys, where there'd be nothing to find until the snow melted, but kept to the route along the streets most of the other kids used.

I came upon Billy Smith making angels on a smooth quilt of snow. He'd lie on his back and move his outstretched arms sidewise, up and down, and spread his legs apart as far as they'd go. When he got up it looked like the outline of an winged angel there in the snow. I snickered because Billy was the farthest thing from an angel I could imagine. I stopped and made a couple of angels, too.

Farther along I stopped and watched Roger Middleton trying to talk a first-grader into putting his tongue on Mrs. Graves' iron fence. The kid wouldn't do it, so Roger coaxed him into spitting on his finger and then touch the fence. Of course, the finger froze onto the iron immediately and the little kid began to cry.

"You can get it loose," Roger shouted, hopping around with glee. "Spit on it. Just keep spitting on it, and it'll come loose."

When I was little an older boy had persuaded me to put my tongue on that fence. I thought I'd never get loose. Some of the skin tore off. My tongue hurt for a month.

What with these and other diversions, I was late to school. Miss Owen scolded me a little, but I could tell she wasn't really angry. She seemed to understand that a boy didn't have so much fresh, deep snow to play in every day.

During the lunch hour Kenneth and I swung by our hideout and picked up our shovels. The slide on the hill behind school might be the best of the whole winter.

When we got there after school, a few kids had already begun using the slide. It extended the length of a shallow arroyo which ran a couple hundred yards from the crest of the hill to the bottom. To use the slide most kids sat on a piece of sheet metal with the front edge turned up. A garden shovel with the handle cut off, like Kenneth's, was better. But last fall I'd found the best of all: a sure-enough grain scoop. The blade was cracked and worn or it'd never have been thrown away. But it was perfect for the slide, wide and flat with plenty of room to sit on.

We climbed through knee-deep snow to the hilltop where the slide began. The bottom of the arroyo was already becoming packed from the kids' rides who'd beat us to the hill. Kenneth went first, shooting away and down with a wild yell.

I sat on the blade of my grain scoop, raised my feet high before me, and began accelerating like a sky rocket down the hill, steering with both hands around the shovel's forward end where the handle had been. The hillside flashed by, faster and faster, and all too soon I streaked into the wide ditch which skirted the bottom of the hill and up the ditch bank and into the air. I landed with a jolt some 20 feet away and then coasted to a stop on the flat beyond.

Kenneth was standing there, grinning and yelling. "Hurry up. Let's go again!"

"A few more times and it'll be really fast," I said.

"Yeah, and tomorrow it'll be icy and we'll *really* fly."

We climbed the hill and rocketed down it again and again until nearly dark. All that week we rejoiced on the hill. The slide became slicker and faster and our flights from the ditch bank carried us ever farther to landings ever harder—until our rear ends were red and sore.

Then on Saturday we joined a gang of kids and shoveled snow from the river ice for skating. It took all morning to clear an area large enough to suit us. That afternoon and for days thereafter whenever we could we played on the ice: hockey, using sticks bent on one end and a crushed tin can, or various games of tag.

By mid-month the cold had retreated. The sun, higher each day above the southern horizon, felt almost hot on my face and began to shrink the deep snow. One night the wind started blowing south across the foothills, heating the air as the wind rasped across the upthrust ridges which extended like fingers from the mountain slopes, eastward onto the plains. It was a chinook wind. It blew all night and into the next day. The wind was warm and smelled like spring a-coming. It sucked at the snow like some giant tongue licking an ice cream cone.

Streets and sidewalks lost their icy covers and the snow blanket disappeared to uncover the brown lawns and dead weeds in vacant lots. From overhead came the cries of northbound geese, vanguard of the coming host of summer birds and insects.

I rejoiced in the stirrings of infant Spring and began to plan adventures unrelated to snow and ice.

It had been difficult for Kenneth and me to continue our protective spying on Miss Owen during the cold spell. But now we took up the task again, convinced our lady was in danger. We saw Dwayne's car parked in front of her house more frequently as the days passed. And the two of them resumed their laughing and talking in the downstairs parlor. But one night when Mrs. Jones left the house for one of her frequent church meetings the lights went on upstairs in Miss Owen's rooms.

As we stood outside in the shadows we could see Dwayne striding back and forth and being charming. And we'd see her pass a window occasionally, looking very happy. Dwayne paused in front of a window.

"Look at him," Kenneth said. "...smiling like one of Mrs. Redd's cats eating a sucker."

"Yeah," I agreed, "he really knows how to spread on the butter and the jam, too. I hope she's not falling for it."

"Well, it looks to me like she's having a good time."

Then the lights went out. We waited to see if she would come out and get in Dwayne's car. We waited a long time. Then he emerged alone, whistling a tune. He jumped in his car and roared away.

One week the talk of our neighborhood was an upcoming movie scheduled for showing Friday through Sunday. We knew it would be the most exciting show ever: "Cimarron," starring Richard Dix. Posters and movie photo scenes displayed each side of the theater entrance promised the greatest ever tale of horses, fighting, adventure. My whole year would be ruined unless I could see that movie. But since the blizzard I'd found no bottles, gunny sacks, nor anything to sell. If only it were summer I could maybe earn a dime by doing an extra good job of mowing Mrs. Bailey's lawn.

Hidden in the back of my dresser drawer were three whole dollars, money given me on birthdays the past two years. One grandmother always sent a dollar and the other 50 cents. But that money was almost sacred. I was saving to buy the most expensive Daisy BB gun in Manning's Hardware Store. Five dollars! And I had resolved never to touch a penny of that money until I had accumulated the entire purchase price.

So, aside from the untouchable BB gun money, all I had was the penny left over from my valentine extravagance. And I wished I hadn't spent that penny at Mrs. Redd's store. The other neighborhood boys had as little cash in hand, or less, than I did. No one had a whole dime for a ticket to the Saturday matinee.

Fortunately, in our neighborhood we had a last resort for such crises, one we'd employed before from time to time. After school one afternoon before the big weekend, a dozen of us gathered in Wilton's garage. It had once been a carriage house but now they called it a garage. There was room for three cars but only one was kept there, a 1928 Essex which was seldom used except on Sundays because walking cost less than gasoline. Inside was a hard-packed dirt floor. We sat on the dirt and explored our desperate situation.

"Who has any money?" I asked. Only four hands went up.

"Well, I've only got a penny," I said.

"I have a penny," Roger Middleton said.

"I have a beer bottle," said Hubert Metnick.

"And I got *two* cents," Davie Kilbourne said proudly, as though he were raising the bet in one of the big poker games downtown.

"Well, *I* got a *nickel*," Scrubby Dillworth announced. We called him Scrubby because he always looked fresh out of the bathtub, well dressed and wearing pretty good shoes.

I'd been keeping track on my fingers. "That makes a dime," I said. "Now all we got to do is choose the one to go."

"Let's spin the bottle," Roger said. "The one it points to gets to go."

"But only the ones with money are in it," Davie said. "And I oughta get two places." We shouted him down.

"Just a minute," Scrubby said. "I'm puttin' in a whole nickel. And I'm not gonna be in any spin the bottle. *I'm* gonna go or I won't put up my nickel. Then what're you gonna do?"

What we wanted to do was tackle Scrubby and punch him good and get him all dirty to run home to his mama. But we knew we'd never learn how the show turned out if we didn't let him have his way. Besides, despite his other shortcomings,

Scrubby was a good story teller, probably better than any of us. So it was agreed, with long faces and vengeful glares, that Scrubby would be our eyes and ears at the matinee.

Saturday was a long day, awaiting the hours to creep by until the show was over late in the afternoon. All of us had been in Wilton's garage for up to an hour, when Scrubby finally came sauntering in. He stood in the middle of our circle where we sat in suspense.

"I just wanna say," he smirked, "*that* was the best movie I ever saw. Too bad you couldn't see it, too."

"Get to the telling," Kenneth shouted, even though he hadn't put in any money.

"Yeah, get going, Scrubby. Or you'll be sorry." Davie shook a clenched fist.

"Okay," Scrubby said. "Here's how it started. There was this beautiful music..."

"Forget the music. Get to the show," Roger yelled.

"I thought you wanted to hear it all," Scrubby said. "Well, it starts with some love stuff and Richard Dix...he's Yancey Cravat...gets married and things you don't want to hear about. But it really starts with they're gonna have a big race. And the ones that get there first get their pick of all this land that belonged to the Indians. And Yancey with his pearl handled six shooters is on his big white horse getting ready to race. He already knows what land he wants. There's a beautiful lady ready to race, too, on her black horse. Then they shoot this cannon and thousands of 'em start away. The lady falls off her horse and Yancey stops to help her even though he's far in the lead and bound to beat everybody to his land."

Cries of disgust at such female treachery interrupted the narration. Then Scrubby talked on for nearly an hour, telling the story of Yancey Cravat, his heroic deeds, his noble acts, and finally, the end.

I had to admit Scrubby told the story well. It was almost as good as being there. Walking toward home, with Paint beside me, I daydreamed of being like Yancey Cravat, riding a big white horse, the sun glinting on my pearl handled six shooters, and how I'd take care of Dwayne Tyler.

Near home Mrs. Bailey's little mutt came running up and started yapping. Paint just ignored it. I kicked at the dog and missed. "Take that, you miserable cur," I said, my lips set in a fierce scowl. "And don't you ever go near Miss Owen again, or I'll..."

Next day after school I walked home with Davie. I started talking about the show.

To my surprise, Davie said, "That Scrubby is the biggest liar ever.

"My sister went to the movie with her boyfriend. And she said after Yancey caught the niterglissen bomb and saved everybody, he never rode off into the sunset with a girl. He died. And there was a lot of other stuff Scrubby made up."

"I didn't like that part anyway," I said. "...about riding off with a *girl*."

"Yeah, but if he lied about that, how much of the rest was lies?"

Next day the word was out and after school we all caught up with Scrubby a few blocks away and circled around him. Davie was elected to take our revenge because he was about Scrubby's size, and besides he was the maddest 'cause he'd put two cents in the pot.

It really wasn't much fun, though. Davie made Scrubby admit his sins, called him a liar, and punched him a couple times. Then Scrubby started crying and we just stood there while he started off toward home. We had to be satisfied with watching him go and yelling, "Run home to your mama, you little panty waist...you bloomer button."

A few days later, after I'd finished my chores, my mother said we had to talk. We sat in the kitchen, and I could tell from her expression she had bad news. She reached out and patted my hand and managed a sad smile.

"Johnny, you remember when I told you about the baby? What you said? That it would be just one more mouth to feed?"

"Yes, Mom. It'll be a problem, won't it? But we'll make out. We always do. *You* always manage. Somehow."

"Somehow. Yes. But now I don't *know* how." She uttered a little sob and then stared out the window. "We've stopped taking the newspaper. And the telephone is gone. That saves a little..."

"Yeah, I guess we're the only kids who don't have a phone. Or the comics in the paper. But that's all right, Mom. Kenneth lets me read his comics. And who needs a phone?"

She sat there, her shoulders slumped, her head hanging down, tears running down her cheeks. I felt awful bad for her. Then I thought of something I'd been meaning to tell her.

"I've got some good news, Mom," I said excitedly. She looked up and brushed away the tears. I took her hand and spoke on. "I've been asking around and there's two kids in my class who get money and food from the government. It's a new thing they call relief. And another boy says his family gets money from the county, too...just for doing nothing. Isn't that great? Why don't *we* get in on that? Then you wouldn't have to worry so much."

My mother sat up straight and proud and said firmly, "Oh, *we* couldn't do *that*."

"Why not?" I asked, puzzled by her reaction to my good news.

"Johnny, that's for people who really *need* help. But not for us."

"Well, don't we need a little help, too?"

"Absolutely not. We're getting along just fine. I know it isn't easy and there's things we can't afford. But we're going to make it ourselves...why my mother and brother would be simply mortified if they knew we were taking relief...or going on the county. And so would your father and I."

She paused, deep in thought, and then went on. "Johnny, you can go back as far as you want in our family and never find one who didn't make his own way...or fail to pay what he owed...no matter how long it took. And we'll do the same. Sometimes I can't pay all the rent when it's due. But I'm keeping track of it. And they'll get every cent we owe just as soon as I can manage.

"Your father is over in South Dakota because he couldn't find a job here and couldn't bear to sit around and take handouts so long as he is able to work." She was silent for a moment and then said, "You *do* understand, don't you Johnny?"

"I...guess so...Mom," I mumbled. It didn't make sense to me not to take any help we could get, but at the same time I felt proud of her and of being part of such a family.

"Thank you, Johnny." She hugged me and then pushed me away and the sad look returned to her face. She said, "Now, there's something else...and it is very hard." She hesitated and I knew she didn't want to tell me. Then she blurted it out. "We can't keep Paint any more."

That was worse than anything I could have imagined—except maybe my father had had an accident or something like that.

"Mom," I wailed. "How can you even *think* that? Why it's getting so warm old Paint sleeps in the shed. He's hardly ever in the house. And I'll keep him outside all the time when the baby comes. And he don't eat much."

"He eats more than you think. I can't let him go hungry. And there won't even be scraps for a while. We have to save more for the baby. The doctor will cost $25. And I don't know *where* we're going to get that. We have to save every penny we can."

She began weeping softly, as though she couldn't cope any more. I felt about as sad as ever in my whole life.

I put my arms around her and said, "There's my three dollars, Mom. We'll use that."

"Oh, we can't. You've been saving so long."

"Who needs a BB gun? I waited this long. I guess I can wait longer."

She put on a brave smile and patted my hand again. "I may have to *borrow* your money...when the baby comes. You think about Paint. And tell me in a day or two."

"Okay, Mom," I mumbled and went outside to ponder the catastrophe that had dropped into my life. Paint was lying near the shed. When he saw me he sat up and grinned and started thumping his big tail on the ground. I kneeled beside him and stroked his fur. The dog knew something was wrong. He whined and snuggled close to me, peering into my eyes, licking me on the cheek, trying to make me get up and run and laugh. But I couldn't.

I tried to think. But all that came into my head were pictures of my dog moping down an alley alone, with nobody to love him. Old Paint. Where could he go? Nobody wanted a dog. Nobody wanted him when he found me. I felt like crying. But I didn't. That'd only make it worse for Mom and for Paint.

The next few days were pretty bad. I felt like I had a load of concrete in my stomach. I felt the sort of deep sorrow I imagined I'd feel if my brother or sister died or something. I couldn't eat much. Miss Owen noticed something was wrong and she tried extra hard to cheer me and asked whether I was sick.

Kenneth knew about the trouble, of course, and we'd sit in our hideout and plot ways to keep our dog. We thought of taking Paint up to Canada and running a trap line, living off the land. We wouldn't have to go to school, and we'd come back in a few years wearing our Eskimo parkas and loaded with money from selling our furs. It would mean leaving Miss Owen and our mothers, but we gloried in talking about how they'd miss us and how proud they'd be when we returned... rich. But we didn't have any traps nor money to buy them and weren't real sure where Canada was.

We went down to the Montgomery Ward store, thinking surely there were jobs in such a big store. The manager laughed and said to come back in a few years. Then one day we found a way. I ran home yelling and happy again for the first time in days. I gave Paint a big hug then bolted for the kitchen door. I couldn't wait to tell my mother. I slammed the door shut, a big smile on my face. My mother returned it. I could tell she felt better already.

"Mom," I gasped, breathless from the run home. "I've got good news about Paint."

"Oh," she said, "hurry and tell me."

"Well, he's almost as much Kenneth's dog as mine. He likes us both. And Kenneth says Paint can stay at *his* house."

She frowned. "Do you think Mrs. Martin will allow it?"

"Kenneth says it's okay with her. And that's enough for me. It'll be almost as good as having Paint here. I'll see him every day. And I'll bring him to see you...and the baby when it comes."

"But will Kenneth's *father* approve?"

"He doesn't know yet. But he's hardly ever home. So he won't mind."

And so I took Paint over to Kenneth's. We kept him in the Martin's garage for several days. Whenever Kenneth let him out, he'd come back to our house. I'd scold him and take him back until he finally understood he was to stay there.

Everything was nearly as good as before, and I figured someday Paint could come back and live with us again. It was just fine except for one thing. Mr. Martin *did* mind. He was a railroad conductor and was gone days at a time. Paint and I were in Kenneth's kitchen the day Mr. Martin came home.

From the way he slammed into the house and scowled around, I figured he'd stopped at one of the saloons on Main Street, which he usually did. He wasn't really a bad man, except when he was drinking...and that seemed most of the time.

He took one look at Paint and yelled, "Get that damn dog out of here! Can't a man come home without finding it like a zoo?"

He raised his hand like he was going to strike Kenneth. Old Paint jumped to his feet and bared his teeth and growled deep in his chest. Mr. Martin jumped back.

"Look at *that*," he shouted. "That mongrel thinks this is *his* house. You get him out of here, boy. And don't bring him in here again or I'll whip you good." We took Paint outside...fast.

"Well, I guess that's that," I said.

"Oh, it'll be all right," said Kenneth, with confidence born of experience. "I'll keep Paint in the garage when my father's home. When he's in town he's either down on Main Street or sleeping. He won't hardly know Paint is here."

I hoped Kenneth was right. And it turned out he *was*—for several months anyway, until a terrible thing happened.

By the end of March things had settled down. The big white dog's gaunt flanks began to fill out. Kenneth's mother gave Paint lots of leftovers from their meals and sometimes even bought bones and meat for him. She didn't have to save her pennies because she wasn't going to have a baby. Besides, whatever his other faults, Mr. Martin made good money for those times.

Near month's end our ice rink cracked and then slowly melted until the river could be seen again, flowing in a channel that widened daily until all the ice was gone. At least once a day I went to the river, and watched the slow dying of winter and the birth of spring. Ahead stretched two long months of school—made more tolerable by afternoons and weekends along the river banks and in the water itself when it warmed enough for swimming.

Chapter Three   April

Fishing season opened April First. I awaited it more impatiently than any other day in the year, except maybe Christmas. After school, one afternoon before opening day, Kenneth and I revisited the places where we'd found bait the year before. We'd sink a spade into the likely spots and then carefully break up the wet, good-smelling clods of earth. In the best places, each shovel we turned over would contain two or three firm, wriggling earthworms a couple inches long.

Paint would watch us. Then he'd start digging his own hole nearby. He'd dig furiously with his front paws and send the dirt flying back between his hind legs. He'd hear the dirt fall behind him and turn quickly, bark, and bite at it. Then he'd turn back to his hole and dig rapidly again, stopping every now and then to stick his head into the hole until his nose became crusted with dirt. We laughed at him.

We put our worms carefully into a can of damp, rotted leaves and kept the can indoors at night. Morning temperatures were still below freezing and we had to keep the worms alive and frisky until the day we would offer them to the fish.

It was hard to sleep Friday night before the season opened. I lay awake and thought of my tackle. I had a flexible steel fishing rod, a fabulous birthday present from my mother the year before when she'd been able to afford $1.50 for a gift. When collapsed the rod was about three feet long. You pulled on the tip end and the middle and top sections came out, like the tubes of a telescope and you had a fine whippy rod nearly nine feet long. For my reel I'd traded a cracked wooden flute that still worked. On the reel was wound thirty feet of genuine enameled fishing line. And I had a dozen or so lead sinkers and half a dozen steel hooks.

I thought about sitting on the river with my line in the water, seeing the line begin to jerk, feeling the fish when it was hooked, and then pulling it up, bright and flopping, onto the river bank. It was like finding buried treasure, I thought. I was awake a long time before I finally dropped off to sleep.

Before daylight I was up and dressed without waking my brother. When I went into the kitchen the light was on. My mother was stirring a bowl of batter.

"Oh, boy. Pancakes," I said.

"And *where* do you think *you're* going at this hour?" she asked. She looked stern, and I wondered how she could have forgotten.

"*You* know, Mom. It's opening day."

"And so it is. But before you go anywhere, young man, there's a few things to be done around here." I looked closely to see if she was serious. She was.

"I want these windows washed inside," she went on. "It's time to wash your bed sheet and clean up that room and closet. They're a fright. Then I want you to take your sister over to the church party."

"But, *Mom*! I'll do it this afternoon, when I finish fishing."

"That's what you always say, Johnny. You know what I tell you about putting things off. They never get done. And I want you to bring in more coal. We're about out."

I looked down at the full bucket near the stove and then up into her face. Her eyes were laughing. She reached out her arms and I ran to her.

"April Fool," she said. "I really fooled you, didn't I?"

"Mom, you had me scared. I almost died."

She hugged me and then spooned batter into the cast iron skillet. A wonderful aroma spread into the air. "There's something else," she said, flipping over the pancakes. "Fishing season has been postponed."

"You're not gonna get me again," I said and sat down at the table. "They wouldn't do that. Would they?"

"No. You're right. But April Fool again, anyway."

I laughed with her.

I left the house, my stomach warm and full, carrying my fishing rod and the can of worms. I started for the river where Kenneth and Paint would meet me at sunup.

But no sun rose that morning. It was cloudy and began snowing lightly before I reached the river. Soft flakes as big as postage stamps fell out of the pinkish sky, as though someone up there was plucking a white goose and letting feathers drift down through the still air. The big snow flakes melted as they reached the warm earth. It would be wet that morning, but not cold. Even if it had been, I was too excited to care. When the fishing season opened, you went fishing, no matter the weather.

I reached the river bank and saw Kenneth and Paint approaching through the falling snow. Paint ran toward me. He slid to a stop and danced around, grinning and wagging his tail. I grabbed him around the neck and wrestled him on the ground for a bit. He was sure glad to see me.

Our fishing place was a strip of grass along the river bank, across the river from the park. The river made a bend there, and steel rails driven into the river bottom held a wall of thick timbers to keep the river from washing out the bank. Along and below the wall for several hundred feet the river had washed a deep hole where the fish were. We called it The Logs. The grassy bank was about five feet above the water. It was a good place for diving and swimming, too, when the water warmed later in spring. Now the water was still icy cold and dark under the snow shedding sky.

We threaded the firm, wiggly worms onto our hooks and cast out into the deep water. We couldn't see the bottom nor any fish. They'd be deep down, near the rocks below the water's surface. Paint sat watching us, his head cocked on one side and then the other, puzzled with this new game we were playing.

"I hope we catch a dozen suckers," Kenneth said. "Or twenty or thirty. Boy, think of all those candy bars."

"We might catch some bullheads, too," I said. "They're good eatin'. But I hope we catch a couple trout. They're in here, you know."

"Yeah. Sometimes in the spring. They're better eatin' than bullheads and better lookin', too."

Nothing happened for quite a spell. I looked at the white feathers floating down onto the water and, across the river, falling down through the skeleton branches of tall cottonwood and boxelder trees and onto the needles of the dark spruce trees in the park.

"Hey, you got a bite!" Kenneth said.

I looked down where my line entered tautly into the water. It moved slightly. I looked at Kenneth's line. "So have you," I said. "We gotta be careful not to pull up too soon. Give 'em time to swallow the bait."

We watched our lines closely, tense with hope. The little nibbling movements progressed into bigger ones. Then my line jerked hard, and I raised the rod high, feeling the solid surge of a fish on the line, from down deep where I couldn't see it.

Kenneth gave a whoop and I saw he had a fish on, too. Suckers don't give much of a fight, and we soon hoisted our fish out of the water and onto the bank. We held them squirming in our hands, comparing them for size. Kenneth's was about 12 inches long, mine a couple inches smaller.

"Golly, mine's a big one," he chortled. "Mrs. Redd oughta give me a candy bar for just one this size."

"Well, she won't. You know her. You oughta be glad it isn't little."

"I bet she'd trade a candy bar for four or five little ones."

"Maybe. She says they make her cats choke."

We thought the catching would speed up after that. But it didn't. A long time passed between bites, while the white feathers kept drifting down, melting on the ground. Kenneth caught two more suckers and I caught one, all about the size of my first one.

"What time do you reckon it is?" Kenneth asked, after a long spell of no action.

"My stomach says it's near noon. I guess we oughta quit." Just then my line gave a little jerk then a big, solid one. I yanked up my pole and felt a strong thrashing something on the line. The pole bent and the line began slicing through the water toward the other bank, my old reel singing clickety-clickety. The line stopped going out and I started reeling it back in. The fish didn't want to come. It pulled and ran and pulled and then jumped clear of the water.

"That's no sucker," I said.

"You bet it isn't. It's a trout all right. Be careful you don't lose him."

I was afraid it'd get off the hook before I even got it close to the bank. I began reeling in the line again, and the fish came with it, thrashing again and again but too tired to pull out the line. I pulled the fish in near the logs and to the surface. It was a trout all right. Taking a deep breath I hoisted it up and onto the grass, where it lay flopping, white bellied and black-speckled with a bright pink band along its sides.

"A *rainbow*!" Kenneth said. "...bigger'n my biggest sucker."

"And won't that make a meal!" I said. "Trout's better eatin' than chicken." I could hardly wait to show my mother. She was always telling me to bring home a trout big enough to bake in the oven, but I knew she didn't really expect me ever to do it.

We fished for quite a long time after that, hoping we'd catch another trout or at least more suckers. But we didn't. The snow stopped falling and a stiff breeze came up. It was very cold then, near the river, in the wind. So we pulled in our lines and agreed to meet that afternoon to trade our suckers to Mrs. Redd. I told Kenneth it would have to be late because I had a lot of work to do.

It was after four when I rode over to Kenneth's house, carrying my two suckers in a little cloth sugar sack. My mother's eyes had nearly popped out of her head when she saw the big trout. She said she'd put bread stuffing inside the fish and bake it. The trout was so beautiful I hated to slit it open and clean it. But I did and then put it on the back porch to keep cold.

We pedaled over to Mrs. Redd's store, with old Paint alongside, making frequent stops to sniff and lift his leg and then run to catch up. The streets were wet and I tried to steer through the driest places so I wouldn't get spattered so much.

Mrs. Redd was waiting on a customer. She looked up and smiled. We examined the candy bars in their rows of boxes until the customer left.

Mrs. Redd said cheerfully, "I bet you boys brought me some fish." We laid our suckers on a paper she spread on the counter. She looked at the big fish and the four smaller ones.

"That don't come out even," she said.

Kenneth held up the big one. "This'n is a whopper, Mrs. Redd. He's worth a candy bar."

"The big un ain't as much as two of t'others," she said. "Business is business. But I'll give you a two-for-a-nickel candy bar and one penny candy for the big fish."

"Okay," Kenneth said glumly. "And I'll take a Butterfinger for the other two. And I guess I'll win me another yo-yo." She put the box of chocolate-covered mints on the counter. Kenneth studied them and selected two. Both had white centers. He groaned and popped one in his mouth. I chose a Baby Ruth for my two suckers.

She put our candy in two little paper sacks. "Bring them fish out back, boys. And I'll call the cats." We followed her to the back of the store and outside.

"Here Kitty, Kitty, Kitty," Mrs. Redd called. Over a dozen cats of every size and color came running from all directions, from the old barn, from the unused chicken coop beside the barn, and from a hole under the back of her store. She maneuvered around and gave a fish to each of five cats and shooed the others away. They went a ways off and stood meowing pitifully.

"These cats won't eat all them fish," she said. "The others'll get some later." One of the cats dragged its fish into the hole beneath the store. Two from the fish-less crowd followed it and there ensued a ruckus of moaning, hissing, and screeching. Two of the cats scrambled back out of the hole.

The other four cats sniffed at their fish and then began tearing away with their sharp little teeth. They chomped fiercely on scales, skin, flesh, and bones. I could hear the bones crack and a crunching noise as they ate into the fish heads.

"Well, boys," said Mrs. Redd, "I got to get back to my store. I don't s'pose I'll see you 'til next Saturday, will I?"

"My mom won't let me fish on Sundays," I said. "But maybe we can catch some after school."

"I'll take all you can catch," she said, "unless it gets to be too many. But I don't think you'll catch *that* many."

She went back into her store in her red dress, red stockings, and red shoes.

Monday dawned clear and sparkling, not at all the kind of day to sit in school and look through windows at the puffy, white cotton-ball clouds go poking along in the clear blue sky. Miss Owen said if I didn't quit looking out the window I'd have to sit with the girls. So I stopped, except when her back was turned to write on the blackboard.

It seemed like a week until the school day ended, but when finally it did, Kenneth and I ran to our homes and got our fishing poles. We met at The Logs, hurriedly baited our hooks and cast into the deep, dark water. We sat side by side. Paint lay on his stomach a few feet away, head on outstretched paws, eyes closed, soaking up the warm sun. It was glorious sitting there, with the gurgle of the river's current washing against the logs, immersed in the aroma of wet spring earth, and watching our lines for the first nibble.

From the corner of my eye I saw Paint lift his head and look behind us. At that instant a big, hard hand grabbed the back of my coat collar and lifted me to my feet. Beside me Kenneth was hoisted up simultaneously. We didn't have to turn our heads to know who'd grabbed us like that.

I heard Dwayne's deep, mean laugh. "I gotcha, you little bastards. Gotcha for sure." He kept on laughing.

I twisted and pulled to get away. Beside me Kenneth was doing the same. But Dwayne was too strong. We couldn't get loose. I heard Paint bark and then he came prancing and dancing alongside, a big grin on his face. He darted away, barking, the way he sounded when we were roughhousing with him. I knew he thought it was just another of those fool games boys played. And he wanted to play, too.

I quit struggling, hoping Dwayne would relax his grip. But he didn't.

"I've seen you little bastards sneaking and peeking around your teacher's house," he said and gave us another shake. "And I'm here to tell you you ain't gonna do it no more. You savvy?"

I nodded and Kenneth said, "Okay."

"But just to make sure you remember, I think I'll give you a little bath. You stink. Don't your mamas ever wash you?"

That made me mad. I kicked back and felt my heel strike his leg.

"Ow! Damn you!" Dwayne said and he shoved me forward and let go my collar.

I fell downward into the water. I went under and deep until I felt the river bottom. I felt the icy shock of the water on my hands and face and then all over me as the water penetrated my clothing. I gave a push with my feet and went upward until my head was above the water's surface and I gasped for air. My heavy shoes and water-logged clothes seemed wanting to pull me down again into the deep. I was so numb and cold I almost didn't care, but I floundered away with my arms and kicked my heavy feet and finally reached the log wall. I fumbled for a steel rail and held on, breathing like I'd just run a mile.

I looked around, expecting to see Kenneth in the water, too. But he wasn't. From up above I heard Dwayne shout, "Come here, you little bastard. I'm gonna *drown* you."

Then I heard Paint snarling and Kenneth shrieking from what seemed a distance away. I heard Dwayne curse and then cry out, "Get away from me! Damn you!" The sound of Paint's growling receded rapidly from the river bank.

I reached out and grabbed a log and began struggling upward, using the spaces between the logs to climb. My numb hands and feet seemed unwilling to work as they should. Slowly up I went, hand over fumbling hand, foot over clumsy foot, my flesh trying to shrink from my icy, water-heavy clothing.

At last I got my head above the top log and held myself there with both hands, my feet in a log space below. Dwayne was running away fast with Paint nipping at his heels.

I heard Kenneth shout, "Paint! Come here, Paint." The dog stopped and watched Dwayne running, then he turned and came growling back.

I pulled myself up onto the grass, trembling in my cold, heavy clothes.

Kenneth came up. "That dirty skunk," he said. "I wouldn't do that to a dog."

I said, "Lucky thing we had our dog. Or you'd have been in there, too." I got to my feet, the cold water streaming from my jacket and pants and squirting from my shoes. I pulled in my fish line.

"I better go home," I said.

"You need me to go with you? Whatcha gonna tell your mother?"

"I don't know. And don't you tell *your* mother or she won't let you come fishing again."

As I slogged home, colder than I'd ever been, I wondered what I *would* say. I couldn't tell what really happened. As feisty as my mother was, she'd probably go tearing right over to Dwayne's house. And he'd likely hurt her. It was best to keep grownups out of things like this. I decided I'd say I leaned over to check my line and fell in the river. It wouldn't be the first time I'd fallen in, one way or another. Mom was in the kitchen when I sloshed in the back door. She was at the stove, her back to me, singing as usual. She turned and her eyes opened wide.

She said, "My goodness sakes alive! What's happened to you *now*? Get those wet clothes off and stand by this stove. You look half dead!"

I stripped to my underclothes and stopped because my sister was peeking in the door. My mother went to the bathroom and came back with a couple of towels and started scrubbing me fiercely. Then she began to cry.

"Every time you go down to that river," she sobbed, "I wonder if you'll ever come back. And someday you won't." She quit crying after while and looked at me sadly as if I were already dead or something.

"Oh, Mom," I said. "It wasn't nothin'. I just got careless and fell in. I'll be more careful. Besides, I'm a good swimmer. That river can't do nothin' to *me*."

"Anything," she corrected me.

She hugged me and then began scrubbing harder than ever with the rough towel.

"Ow! That hurts," I complained.

"You deserve something that hurts worse," she scolded. "...scaring me like this."

We ate the trout for supper. And it *was* better than chicken which we didn't have but seldom because it was too expensive.

At the table my sister smirked and acted smart. "Quack. Quack," she kept saying. "Johnny thinks he's a duck."

And my mother would say, "Hush up. Eat your supper."

My brother mostly just grinned knowingly. He'd been there before. Once he said, "Next time you oughta take off your clothes. It's easier to swim that way."

After school for a week before my birthday I asked my mother if there'd been any letters for me. She knew why I was asking and each day she'd sadly say no. As my day drew near I began to fear my grandmothers had forgotten. Or maybe they were as hard up as we were and couldn't send any money. But at my birthday dinner there on my plate were three envelopes addressed to me. A letter from my father said now I was twelve he expected I would help my mother more and if he sold a light plant he'd send me a present. In the other envelopes were a dollar from one grandmother and 50 cents from the other.

I was so elated I didn't care if there were any other presents. But my brother gave me six fishhooks and my sister Anna gave me a watch fob my mother had helped her crochet with red string. I said it would come in handy someday when I got a watch. My mother gave me a box of fudge made with cocoa and sugar. It was the best candy ever, even better than a Baby Ruth candy bar. I decided to hide what fudge I didn't have to share with Ralph and Anna and eat one piece a week until it was gone. After dinner there was Happy Birthday singing over a cocoa cake with cocoa icing. I kept thinking I was only 50 cents away from my BB gun.

One Friday evening the last week in April Kenneth and I joined with some neighborhood kids after supper to play Kick The Can. The air that night was so warm I didn't need a jacket. It was almost like summer. Kenneth had left Paint shut up in the garage, because he just couldn't seem to get the hang of how to play the game. He'd keep running around our hiding place, barking, and we'd always get caught.

Kick The Can was sort of like Hide And Go Seek, but a lot more fun. We'd put an empty can under the arc light on the corner. One kid was chosen to be "It," and the rest of us went different directions and hid. When the kid who was "It" found one of us, he would race back to the can. If he got there first he'd call out the name of the one he'd found, and that kid had to stay in jail under the arc light. The object was to get everyone in jail. Then someone else had to be "It."

The game really got exciting when several kids were in jail. Because if someone could sneak in—while "It" hunted another victim—and kick the can off into the dark, then everyone got out of jail and ran off to hide again. "It" had to retrieve the can, set it under the arc light, and start all over. You had to be very crafty and a fast runner to get everyone in jail. And not many ever did it.

Kenneth and I were hiding in a clump of Bridal Wreath bushes in Roger Middleton's back yard when we began to tire of the game. Hubert Metnick was "It." He was a very slow runner and not at all crafty. He'd hardly get one or two kids in jail before someone would run in and kick the can.

"I know something that'd be a lot more fun than this," I whispered.

"What?"

"Let's get our bikes and ride up to the bluff and see if Dwayne is parking there with one of his girls...and pester him."

"Do you think we dare? It'll make him awful mad."

"How's he gonna know who it is in the dark? Besides, he owes me one."

"Okay," said Kenneth. "I'm game."

So we pedaled our bikes past The Logs, over the river bridge, through the park, and up the long road that climbed to the bluff. At the top, along the brow of the bluff, tall sagebrush bushes grew around a barren, rocky area. And at the bluff's edge the ground dropped steeply down to the river below. It was a favorite parking place for the few young men who owned or could borrow a car.

We left our bikes in a clump of sagebrush and quietly approached the parking area. We could see in the darkness, lit only by starlight, one car. It was Dwayne's Ford. We went closer until we heard a noise from inside the car. It was a girl's giggle. Then we heard Dwayne's deep voice but couldn't make out the words. We crouched and crept behind the car until we could almost touch it. We knelt down, each one alongside a rear wheel. The car windows were down.

"You know it's true, Aggie," came Dwayne's pleading voice. "I love only you. Cross my heart."

"Oh, yeah. Then why is it you only take me out once in a while?"

"I take you out as often as I can."

"Tell it to the marines! I've seen you night after night with other girls."

"My aunt...she don't want me to go with the same girl all the time. She says I'm too young to go steady."

Silence for a while. I could hear the frogs chirping away down near the river.

"I promise, Aggie. It's really only you I love. Now, come on. Give us a little kiss."

I heard a squirming and twisting of bodies on the car seat, then her voice, protesting. "You said a little *kiss*. That don't give you any right to..."

"Ah, now, Aggie. What's the harm? You let me before."

"Well..."

Silence. Then more squirming noises. I tossed a pebble at Kenneth. It was time. Each of us began pounding on a rear tire with the fist-sized rocks we'd picked up on the road below the bluff.

Bump. Bump. Bump.

"What's that noise?" the girl shrilled.

"Damn!" said Dwayne and flung open the car door on his side. But we had already run quietly away and hid behind a tall sagebrush. We could barely make out his shadowy form as he looked around. He walked around the car and looked beneath it. Then he got back in the car.

We waited until we heard her giggle again and the sound of their voices. We crept behind the car and waited until they quit talking and all was silent. Then we waited a while longer before we began pounding on the tires again.

Bump. Bump. Bump.

"Somebody's out there," the girl shrieked.

"I'll *kill* 'im," Dwayne shouted and flung open his door.

This time we were a little slow on our getaway and had just started off, Kenneth in one direction and I in another.

"Watch out, Henry," I shouted.

"This way, George," Kenneth yelled.

Dwayne pounded along after me until he tripped and fell. He cursed bitterly. Then he stood up and peered around while I lay on the ground behind a big sagebrush, barely able to see him silhouetted against the sky a few yards away.

"You little bastards," Dwayne yelled. "I know who you are. You can't fool me with that Henry and George stuff. Wait'll I catch you one of these days. You'll wish you was never borned."

After while he returned to the car. I heard their voices, arguing. Then he started the car. The lights went on, and the car backed up and then swung off down the road toward the park, the rear wheels spitting clouds of dust and rock.

Kenneth and I met at our bikes. We laughed and hit each other playfully.

"Boy, was *he* mad!" Kenneth chortled.

"Yeah, we really got him *that* time."

"Do you think he knows it was us, Johnny?"
"Naw. How could he? It was too dark."
"I hope he couldn't. It was bad enough before."
"We just got to keep clear of him, Kenneth. That's all."

We didn't go back through the park. We rode down the other side. It was a long way home, and my mother was sitting on the front porch swing waiting for me.

After the night when we heckled Dwayne up on the bluff, we kept an eye out for him at all times. His natural mean streak would be the meaner for his believing we were "sneaking and peeking," as he'd put it. And suspecting we were the ones who spoiled his fun with Aggie was, for Dwayne, the same as *knowing* it was true for certain. So, continuing our vigilance over Miss Owen, we became extra cautious, not riding past her house during the daytime, conducting our observations as stealthily as Cheyenne Indians, or so we imagined.

One evening, we ditched the street corner game again, and rode over to Miss Owen's street. We left the bikes half a block away and kept in the shadows up to her house. Dwayne's car was parked out front. No lights showed downstairs so we figured Mrs. Jones was at another church meeting. Upstairs both rooms Miss Owen rented were lighted.

Hidden in the gap between two big spruce trees, we saw through a window Miss Owen rise and go into the next room. Dwayne got to his feet, turned off the light and followed her. We crept along the side of the house to the back yard. From the rear of the lot we could see up into what we thought was Miss Owen's bedroom. They stood close to each other. Suddenly Dwayne grabbed her and began kissing her. She seemed to yield at first then she pushed him away and turned her back to him.

"How can she stand for him to touch her?" Kenneth whispered.

"I don't know. It seems like grownups don't have good sense about things like that."

"Look, Johnny. He's going over by the door." The light went out.

"We oughta throw a rock through the window or something," I said. "...then let the air out of his tires."

"Hey, the light's back on. She turned it on. See her standing there by the door?"

Her face looked angry. She seemed to be shouting at Dwayne. He walked to her and slapped her hard. He put his face close to hers and seemed to be saying something. Then he walked out the door. Pretty soon we heard the front door slam shut, his footsteps on the sidewalk, then his car started and zoomed away.

Miss Owen still stood by the door, her head down, her shoulders shaking. She raised her head and we could see she was crying.

"That dirty coyote," Kenneth said. "He oughta be whipped."

"Yeah. I wish I was big enough to do it. I wish both of us could do it."

"We could tell the police."

"They wouldn't listen to us. They'd probably put us in jail for watching."

"Well, what good is it to love her from afar and not be able to protect her?"

"I don't know, Kenneth. But we gotta try. We took our oath, remember?"

"Maybe we could put water in his gas tank. That'd slow him down for a while."

"Good idea," I said. "But maybe now she knows how bad he is she won't let him come and see her."

We went back through the shadows to our bikes and pedaled slowly back to the neighborhood, wishing we were Yancey Cravat or Robin Hood. Then we'd fix old Dwayne for good, so's he wouldn't bother Miss Owen or us ever again.

Chapter Four   May

It was May First; May Day, when kids placed on front doorknobs little paper baskets containing spring blossoms—and candies, too, if they could afford them.

In school Miss Owen had us make baskets out of colored paper. She showed us how to roll the paper and paste the edges to make a cone, then make a paper loop and paste that onto the open end of the cone.

Gwendolyn Chesley kept looking back at me from her seat near the front of the room. I'd look away fast and when I glanced back she'd be smiling like Mrs. Redd's cats eating suckers and I'd look away again. I just knew she was planning to hang a May basket on the doorknob at my house, knock, and run off...but not very fast. If I caught her, which I could easily do as fast as *she'd* run, then I was supposed to kiss her. But I planned not to be home until near dark. Maybe my brother would chase her. But I knew he wouldn't. She was too young for a big high school fellow to chase down the street. Now if it was Maxine Wilton, he might chase *her*. But not Gwendolyn.

Miss Owen had seemed subdued and sad since that night Kenneth and I had seen her crying. But helping us make the May baskets seemed to perk her up, and before the afternoon was over she was almost her old self: smiling, laughing, excited about this "other day for lovers," as she kept calling it.

I hurried home after school and told my mother I'd be back in time for supper. I got my bike and started quickly for Kenneth's house to get away before Gwendolyn showed up. In his garage we had our May basket for Miss Owen. It was just a piece of white cardboard folded into a triangle with the edges glued and a piece of string poked through the cardboard for a handle. It wasn't as colorful as the ones Miss Owen taught us to make, but after we'd put in a lilac bloom and a few bright yellow violas it was mighty pretty. In the bottom were half a dozen jelly beans and a piece of paper on which we'd printed "for Miss Owen from Sir Morgan and Sir Benneville." We put the basket in a brown grocery sack so's no one would see what we were up to. Old Paint whined and whined when we shut the garage door on him. He wanted to go awful bad, but we couldn't have him along on such a secret mission.

We pedaled over to Miss Owen's street and left our bikes about half a block from her house. Dwayne's car wasn't there. He didn't seem to come around much in the daytime.

We approached cautiously. Near the house we looked all around. Nobody in sight. We tiptoed up the steps, hung the basket on the doorknob, pounded on the door, and ran away fast. We didn't expect her to chase us but we didn't want her to *see* us either. We stopped behind a lilac hedge two houses away, where we could peer through the branches and see her door. After quite a while the door opened and old Mrs. Jones came out. She looked around then picked the basket off the doorknob and went back in the house. We were disappointed but we grinned at each other and started back to our bikes.

We pedaled slowly toward our neighborhood, basking in thoughts of May Day, the "other day for lovers," feeling the warmth of the late afternoon, immersed in the sweet smell of lilacs which thrust their lavender blossoms from bushes all along our way.

The next Saturday morning my brother Ralph and I were put to spading the garden plot out in the back yard where my mother would plant radishes, carrots, string beans, cucumbers, winter squash, potatoes, and cabbage. Around the edge of the garden she would plant her flowers—yellow and orange calendulas and nasturtiums, bright and perky rose moss, red and pink zinnias, and in the back, to climb up a chicken wire fence, fragrant, colorful sweet peas. We needed the vegetables, but my mother always wanted the flowers, too. She said our lot was so plain it needed flowers.

I looked at the area we had to dig and groaned. It looked as though it would take all day, and I wished it was already done, the vegetables ready to eat and the cucumbers made into dill pickles. But that would be near the end of summer, and I shouldn't wish away a summer that hadn't even come.

Ralph beat me to the spading fork so I had to use the shovel. He measured off 25 paces wide and 30 deep. He drew a line in the dirt with his foot.

"That's your half." He pointed. "And this is mine." He started spading, sinking the fork into the ground, turning over each forkful and breaking up the clods.

"Are you sure that's half? Your part looks smaller than mine."

"Measure it yourself then." He kept working. He almost had a row finished already.

"If you find any worms, save 'em for me," I said.

"I'm not wasting time on worms. I got a date with Maxine this afternoon. And I'm gonna get done before then."

I placed the point of my shovel in the dirt and jumped on the flanges with both feet. The shovel sank into the soft earth. I hauled back on the handle, turned the blade over and broke up the clump. I groaned, thinking of how many shovels I'd have to turn before I finished.

"This shovel is hard to use," I complained. "When you finish halfway, I get to use the fork."

"The way you're going, I'll be finished before you're started."

Every couple of shovels I turned I'd find a worm or two and put them in my bait can. For me it was slow going. Ralph was way ahead of me. Every now and then when I stooped to get a worm, I'd pick up a little clod and throw it at him. It would splatter on the back of his shirt.

He'd turn, angry. "Can't you forget you're still a little kid?"

"Well, if I had the fork I could go as fast as you," I'd say.

I spotted a rock in the next shovel I turned. I picked it up and threw it. He was bent over to lift the fork and the rock hit him smartly on the seat of his pants.

"Ow!" he yelled. "*That* does it." He picked up the rock and threw it at me. I ducked but it was high anyway, and it flew over the fence and crashed through a window in the neighbor's house. Splinters of glass tinkled to the ground. Ralph stared open-mouthed and wide-eyed. A moment of silence. Then the neighbor's door flew open and Mrs. Klein came tearing out to the fence, wailing and screaming. She was furious. If she'd been a mad dog, she'd a been foaming at the mouth.

"You little devils! Lookit what you done to my winder."

From our house my mother came running to learn what was the ruckus. She went over to Mrs. Klein and after while calmed her down a bit.

"You're gonna pay for that winder," Mrs. Klein said fiercely. "Them kids is always up to some devilment. Lucky for you it was one of them little winders on the porch 'stead of the big one in the kitchen."

"I'm dreadfully sorry, Mrs. Klein. But we'll take care of it. You know we will."

"Well, you better or I'm gonna call the police." She blustered and complained on and on. My mother listened and soothed her and finally Mrs. Klein went back in her house, muttering about "them little devils" all the way.

Our mother turned from the fence, tears running down her cheeks.

"Oh, boys," she sobbed. "How could you do it? There goes a dollar we can't afford."

"I'm awful sorry, Mom," Ralph said. "I shouldn't got so mad at Johnny."

"Sorry doesn't raise a dollar," she moaned. Ralph put his arms around her. I felt so bad I didn't know what to do.

"It's my fault, Mom. I threw the rock first."

"Well..." she sighed. "That's one thing I can count on. Whenever there's trouble you're in on it." She quit crying and put on her stern look. "Now, Johnny, you march into the house. You can help with the washing until Ralph finishes. Then you can finish your part."

On the kitchen floor was the washtub of soapy water and her scrub board.

"I'll do the scrubbing, Mom. You sit down and rest." I began rubbing a shirt on the corrugated surface of the board. "And I'll pay for the window, Mom...out of my BB gun money."

"Oh, Johnny. You've been saving so long." She sat on the chair looking very sad. "But I might have to borrow it from you."

"Sure, Mom. Anyway, I don't have enough for the gun I'm gonna buy...someday."

It was late afternoon before I finished in the garden. Then I took my fishing rod and bait can and walked down to The Logs. Kenneth was sitting on the bank, Paint snoozing on the grass beside him.

"Where you been?" he said. "I been here a long time. I caught two suckers. But no trout." Paint jumped up and licked my hand and danced around me like he always did.

"I had a little trouble," I said. I baited my hook, cast my line into the deep water and sat down on the bank. I began to feel better, hearing the water gurgle against the log wall, watching little sparrows flitting around in the trees across the river. Before we quit fishing Kenneth caught another sucker and I caught one."I'll loan you one of my suckers," he said. "And we can each get a candy bar from Mrs. Redd."

"I wish she'd give me a nickel instead," I said. "I need it." Then I told him about the broken window. But I didn't tell him about my money. Someday when I had enough I would buy that BB gun. Then I'd casually bring it out. And wouldn't Kenneth's eyes bug out?

That night I took two 50-cent pieces from the place where I hid my money and gave them to my mother for the broken window. She accepted the coins with tears and said she'd return the money when she could. I told her it didn't matter. It would only put off buying the BB gun a while longer.

The next Saturday morning Kenneth and I caught six suckers. And that afternoon when we'd traded them to Mrs. Redd for two candy bars and several bones for Paint, we decided we'd take our slingshots to the old street car barn and try to shoot a few pigeons.

We'd made our slingshots from a forked tree branch with a two-inch, straight handle below the fork. The best ones were shaped more like the letter "U" than the letter "Y." Boxelder trees were a good source of the slingshot crotches, but the best came from ash trees, although a perfect ash crotch was harder to find. To the top end of each crotch we attached a half-inch-wide band of rubber innertube about a foot long. Then we attached one side of a soft leather patch cut from an old shoe tongue to the middle of the rubber band. You'd hold the crotch with the outstretched left hand, put a stone in the patch and draw it back to the right ear with the right hand, aim and let fly. That's how we did it.

The streetcar line had been installed before I was born, when our little town was expected to grow a lot faster than it ever did and before its citizens started acquiring automobiles. The tracks started at a big brick building on the northwest edge of town where the two streetcars spent the nights. The rails ran east from there to the north end of Main Street and then south far beyond where any houses had ever been built. The streetcars were long gone somewhere. But the big old barn still was used for storing trucks and other stuff owned by the town. We knew there was seldom anyone in the barn and never on weekends.

In front, where the rails ran into the barn, were two huge doors which once had opened for the cars. There were no windows on the building's sides. In back was an attached lean-to shed with windows along its upper roof line. High up near the peak of the main building's roof was another row of windows, broken. Through these openings swarms of pigeons flew in and out. Inside was a regular pigeon city.

Kenneth and I shinnied up the boxelder tree, which had handily volunteered to grow alongside the shed in back, and stepped off onto the shed roof. Paint whined and jumped, trying to follow us up the tree. I scolded and ordered him to lie down. He did after a bit but kept on whining, his nose on his paws, tilting his head to look accusingly up at us. The latch was broken on one of the windows where the shed roof joined the main building. Through that window we crept and then slid down a post to the floor inside.

The old barn smelled musty like any place that isn't occupied. The liquid sound of pigeons cooing filled the barn, like the murmurings of ghosts or spirits. It was gloomy and spooky, the little light supplied only by the few windows in back and cracks in the big front doors. I sure wouldn't have gone in there alone.

All manner of boxes and crates were piled everywhere. In the middle, two rail tracks ran over a pit in which I supposed men had once stood to repair the cars overhead. Another smaller pit to one side held a huge rusting furnace.

An occasional small flight of pigeons flew in or out through the broken windows. And once our eyes adjusted to the gloom we could make out hundreds of pigeons, perched here and there high up on the roof beams and braces, peering nervously down at us, heads moving from side to side. Every now and then one or two would take wing and fly out the exit.

We dug in our pockets for the quarter-size rocks we'd gathered for the hunt. One at a time we'd load a rock into our slingshots' leather patches, draw back the rubber innertube bands and let go. Mostly we missed. The rocks would sail up, hit the roof with a loud report you'd think could be heard all the way to the county courthouse and then go ricocheting off and down to fall with another thump. It made quite a racket inside but I doubted it could be heard from without. At least no one had ever come to investigate while we were there.

After a couple of shots Kenneth knocked down a pigeon. Then I got two more. By this time most of the birds were flying, first from one perch to another, then swirling around, dodging the ceiling braces, and finally streaming out through those high up openings. We picked up the three birds and started for where we'd come in.

On the way I spotted a pigeon nest in the sharp angle of a beam brace. I shinnied up a post which descended to the floor and looked in the nest. Inside was a baby pigeon about the size of my fist, without feathers but with beak wide open, begging for a meal. I carefully put the little creature in my jacket pocket, descended back to the floor and showed it to Kenneth.

"What do you want that for?" he asked.

"It's for our zoo...if we ever get one."

"What you gonna call it?"

I thought for a moment. "I think I'll call her Miss Gilmore, like in the comics."

"How do you know it's a her?" Kenneth scoffed.

"Well, I guess I oughta know a girl from a boy, Kenneth."

"Yeah, but how?"

"I don't know. But anyway her name is gonna be Miss Gilmore."

Kenneth shook his head and we started again to our exit. On the ground outside Paint still lay in the dirt. At first he scarcely even looked at us, acting hurt, like he didn't love us any more. But old Paint could never stay sore for long. And pretty soon he was up and dancing all around us with that big old grin, stopping now and then to sniff at the dead pigeons.

As we started for home, Kenneth said, "Do you really eat those pigeons?"

"Sure enough. Why pigeons are real special in fancy restaurants, don't you know? They call 'em squabs and serve 'em under a glass...whatever that is."

"And your mother cooks 'em for you?"

"Of course. She cooks anything I bring home. Unless it's a snake or something like that. Rabbits. Squirrels. Pigeons. So long as I clean 'em."

"I wish my mother would cook pigeons," Kenneth said. "But she won't. I asked her."

"Well, you'll just have to come over to my house for supper some time and see how good pigeons are when my mother cooks 'em."

We got on our bikes and pedaled away, the dead pigeons in a sack and little Miss Gilmore squirming around in my pocket.

Finally it was the last of May and the last week of school. I almost liked school...a little...because it was about over and summer was near with three long months to do whatever I liked. I wouldn't even mind doing my chores. But I would miss seeing Miss Owen. She told us she might go to her home town for the summer but she'd probably return in the fall. I'd be in seventh grade then, but I could still see her and love her from afar.

Something seemed troubling her that last week. She wasn't so joyful. I hoped it was because she would miss Sir Morgan and Sir Benneville or maybe because old Dwayne had finally got her goat. At least she wouldn't be seeing him if she left town.

That week Miss Owen told about an eclipse of the sun that would happen toward week's end. She told us how the moon would move in front of the sun and blot out its light and it would be dark for a while in the daytime. She showed us how to put candle smoke on a piece of glass to look through while the moon moved until it covered the sun. She said that would protect our eyes from being burned.

The night before the eclipse, the Kick-The-Can game was a little more interesting than usual, and it was late when Kenneth and I rode our bikes toward Miss Owen's house. There wouldn't be many more times to check on her. The thought saddened me, even with end of school and summer vacation so near.

We stopped in the shadows a few houses away. Dwayne's car was parked in the street. He was just climbing into the seat. No lights showed in Miss Owen's house, upstairs or down.

The car's engine started and the lights came on. Through the car's rear window we saw no one in the passenger seat.

"I guess she wasn't home," I said.

"Or maybe she's scrunched down in the seat so's nobody will see her."

"Let's follow and see where he goes."

"We'll never be able to keep up. He drives so fast."

But that night Dwayne drove slowly enough so that by pumping hard we could keep his tail light in sight. He didn't drive up to Main Street nor to any of his girl friends' houses. He just drove around for a while as though going nowhere in particular. And then he headed for the river, crossed the bridge and into the park. We figured he was heading for the bluff. Maybe Miss Owen *was* scrunched down in the seat.

Instead of taking the turn up to the bluff, though, the car turned off on a road along the river bank beyond the park to a turn-around beneath the bluff.

We hadn't followed very far when Kenneth gasped, "Stop, Johnny. I'm plumb out of breath." We were both panting from the chase.

"Besides," Kenneth said, "when he reaches that turn-around he has to come this way and he'll likely run over us."

"We'll pull our bikes into the willows if we see him coming back. What d'you suppose he's doing? He never comes in here."

"Let's ditch our bikes and go on foot so's we can hide if we need to."

We walked down the road, listening for the sound of Dwayne's car, watching for headlights coming our way. But we heard or saw nothing until through the dim night, lit only by the stars, we made out the shape of Dwayne's car parked near the river, the lights off. We crept closer until we could make out a dark form at the river's edge.

"What's he doing?" Kenneth whispered.

"Looks like he's pushing something in the water. A roll of something. Maybe a rug."

"It's probably something he stole. He doesn't want to get caught with it."

"We better hide," I said, "...before he comes back."

A few minutes later we heard the car start and then come slowly along the road with the lights off. The car's shadowy bulk inched past where we hid in the willows. We stayed there until we could no longer hear the engine. We walked slowly back to find our bikes.

"What d'you suppose he's up to?" Kenneth said.

"I don't know. To no good, you can bet."

We rode slowly back to town, too puzzled to talk.

Next morning Miss Owen wasn't in our classroom when the school bell rang. Pretty soon old Miss Glanz, the principal, came in.

"Your teacher just didn't show up today," she said. "No notice or anything. Maybe she thinks the school year is already over."

A few kids snickered at her feeble joke.

"I'll stay with you pupils until the substitute teacher arrives. For now, you can study your spelling books."

Half an hour later the substitute came in. She was a cranky old thing. We'd had her once before when Miss Owen was sick. She would crack a boy with her ruler for the slightest disturbance. She never hit the girls. I wished Miss Owen would come back.

As I walked home for lunch the sunlight had a strange and eery cast. It was different than the day before, as though it was coming through a filter of some kind. I supposed it might have something to do with the eclipse, but it seemed ominous and made me feel strange and sad.

That afternoon the cranky old substitute let us go out in the schoolyard to watch the eclipse. We watched the sun through the smoked pieces of glass Miss Owen had helped us make, watched while the light became ever more strange and dim. And the black edge of the moon moved over the sun's orb and kept moving until the sun was blotted out entirely and it was dark, or almost dark, just as Miss Owen had said it would be. We watched while the moon continued to slide and gradually the sun was uncovered again. But the light still had a weird and fearsome quality. I wondered where Miss Owen had gone.

Just before the school bell rang that afternoon, old Miss Glanz came into our classroom again. She looked even more severe than ever, and she usually looked as though she expected the end of the world any moment. She stood behind Miss Owen's desk and coughed. Her hands were shaking. Then she spoke.

"Children, I don't know whether I'm the one to tell you this. But somebody has to. And you'll find out anyway. So maybe it's best you hear it from me and not in bits and pieces and half of it wrong."

She paused and coughed again and fidgeted with her hands.

"Miss Owen will not be coming back to school." Miss Glanz put her handkerchief to her eyes. "Her body was found in the river early this afternoon. The authorities believe she may have taken her own life. That is all anyone knows. Now go on home and try not to think about it."

As I trudged toward home with Kenneth I felt as though only part of me was alive. The words from Miss Glanz had been like a kick in the stomach. I felt afraid and sick but not the kind of sick that calls for castor oil.

"You want to go to our hideout?" Kenneth said.

"Naw. I want to go home, Kenneth."

"I do, too." We walked in silence for another block then he said, "Why do you 'spose she did it?"

"I don't know."

"We didn't do very good at protecting her."

"No. We bitched it up."

"Well, so long," Kenneth said and turned off toward his house.

Two days later the school year ended. Ahead were three glorious months of summer vacation from books and school bells. Kenneth and I should have been happy as two sparrows in a grain bin. But Miss Owen's death haunted us. Instead of running and shouting to celebrate our freedom, we plodded silently away from the school to our secret hideout. We wriggled through the hole in the lilac hedge and laid in the sun on a stack of planks, too depressed even to plan how we'd spend the next day.

Kenneth broke the silence. "Did you see that about Miss Owen in the newspaper last night?"

"We don't take the paper. *You* know that...what did it say?"

"Well, it said she was going to have a baby. And so she drowned herself."

I said nothing, just turned over on the plank so I wouldn't have to look at him.

After while Kenneth said, "Why'd she do it? It's not so terrible to have a baby. Lots of women her age have 'em."

"Yeah," I said, "But if they're not married the other women won't even speak to 'em. And she'd lose her job. Probably never could be a teacher again."

"Well, she could have gone away somewhere...where nobody knew her...and say her husband had died or something. She could have done something besides drown herself, couldn't she?"

Another long silence followed. Then the germ of a thought in my head multiplied until my brain felt feverish with a dark suspicion.

"What if she *didn't* drown herself?" I said.

Kenneth sat up as if I'd poked him with a sharp stick.

"What do you *mean*? They *said* she did."

"But what if she *didn't*? What if somebody *else* did it?"

I turned and looked at Kenneth. His eyes opened wide as the germs of my idea began stirring in his brain, too.

"Who would do *that*?"

I wondered if the fear showed on my face like it did on his.

"Maybe it was...Dwayne," I said. "You remember the night before they found her and we followed him to the river... down below the bluff?"

"He shoved something in the water. We thought maybe it was a roll of carpet."

I sat up. We stared at each other as the possibility became belief. I felt cold and afraid, contemplating such an evil thing and knowing it was not only possible but probable.

"But what can *we* do?" Kenneth pondered, fear in his voice. "Why he'd *kill* us if we said a word about it. And who'd believe two kids?"

"Yeah. We gotta keep quiet. And not tell *anybody*. He'd kill us for sure."

We stayed there a long time, until the sun sank low, and although the afternoon was still warm, I was shivering, thinking of Miss Owen cold in the river.

The next morning I didn't rise with the sun as I usually did. I stayed in bed even after Ralph got up and dressed. I lay there until my mother called out, "Breakfast's ready."

She'd fixed pancakes with wild plum jam, one of my favorites. But I only ate three. After Ralph and Anna left the table, I just sat there. Usually I was the first finished and first to run out of the house. My mother stood beside me and patted my head.

"What on earth is wrong with you?" she asked. "I thought you'd be up and at 'em today...first day of summer vacation. Are you sick?"

"No, Mom. I just feel awful sad."

"Is it because of your teacher? A horrible thing...for one so young."

I nodded. Then I said, "Mom, if you knew something terrible someone did, should you tell somebody else about it?"

She sat down and took my hand, looking thoughtful, as she always did whenever I asked a hard question and she didn't want to give a wrong answer.

"Well, that depends, Johnny. First you must be very sure that what you think you know is true...so you don't falsely accuse someone. And there are different kinds of terrible. Can you be more specific?"

"I guess not, Mom. I need to think about it more."

"Why don't you go fishing? It's *such* a lovely day. Don't spend it moping around the house. I might put you to work." She laughed and stood up. "But be careful of that river. Don't fall in."

I went out to the shed, got my pole and bait can and went to The Logs. I cast my line into the deep water and waited for it to become taut, the bait on the bottom. I wondered if Kenneth and Paint would show up. I wished I had gone by and got them.

It was warm, sitting on the bank in the sun. Song sparrows and tiny warblers were singing away like it was the best day ever. I hadn't slept well and felt myself growing drowsy. I heard a car door close, kind of quiet like, over on the graveled street. Something urged me to look back to see who it was. I jolted wide awake. It was *Dwayne*, coming toward me.

I dropped my pole on the ground and rose to my feet. He waved and grinned. I remembered when he used to walk beside me and trip me. I started backing away along the river's edge to keep a safe distance between us.

"Hi," he called, "I came to give you something." Out of a back pocket he took a slingshot and waved it. It was a good one. I'd seen him knock down robins from the top of a giant cottonwood tree with it.

"I don't use it anymore since I got my rifle," he said. "And I thought maybe you'd like to have it."

I kept backing away as he approached.

"Whatsa matter?" he said. "Don't you want it?"

Something came over me and fear was replaced with a burning hatred, as I studied his grinning, cunning, evil face. It was like I had to vomit. I couldn't stop myself.

"You *did* it, didn't you? *You* killed Miss Owen!"

He stopped as if I'd shot him; his grin vanished. I was so angry I lost all caution.

"We *seen* you!" I screamed. "We seen you shove her into the river."

On his face came that crazed look he'd had the day he killed the cat in his cardboard castle. He took a rock from his pocket and fitted it in the slingshot patch. I turned and began running, zigzagging to spoil his aim. I heard the rock go whizzing by my head. I ran faster, along the river bank, hoping to reach the willows that grew thickly beyond the grass strip bordering The Logs before he nailed me with a rock that likely could kill me. Another rock went zinging past my shoulder and caromed off the ground in front of me. A third rock grazed my left arm and then I was on the path through the willows, running, running. I heard him thrashing along behind. It was slower for him because he had to thrust aside the willows that arched over the path while I could run beneath them.

I stopped to get my breath. The sound of Dwayne crashing along the path was farther behind. I was gaining on him. Then I ran on. The willows thinned out and I knew I was at the north edge of town. I ran into a pasture and saw on my right the rear of the old streetcar barn. I headed for it. I hoped to climb the boxelder tree and get inside the barn before Dwayne came out of the willows and spotted me. Maybe he'd figure I had doubled back through the willows toward town.

Inside the barn I collapsed onto the dusty concrete floor. It seemed I'd never stop panting. I cussed myself for losing my temper and telling Dwayne we'd seen him that night. The fear returned, magnified by being alone in the old barn, the pigeons making their sounds of spirits moaning. I lay there a long time and began to think maybe I'd lost Dwayne. Then I heard a scrambling on the shed's steel roof and knew I'd have to hide somewhere in the barn.

I searched frantically about, rejecting half a dozen hiding places. I heard a noise at the back of the barn and saw a big guy who could only be Dwayne coming through the window and then heard a thump as he slid down the post to the floor.

I felt giddy, faint and hopeless, almost resigned to what would happen when he caught me. Then I thought of Miss Owen and determined that I would not give up so easy. I crept around in the gloom of the barn looking for a place that even if he found me he couldn't get at me. I looked down into the old furnace pit and spied just the place: the old rusty steam tank. I took the stairs down into the pit and saw that the access hole to the tank was open. I scrambled through it and crept back as far as I could. Faint light outlined the opening. Inside was total darkness. The air stank of dirt and rust. I shivered and listened.

"Johnny. Oh, *John-nee-ee-ee*. You in here?" His voice came from near the back. Then I heard his footsteps and crates being moved about as he searched. And then I held my breath. I heard him climb down into the pit, open the furnace door, and poke around inside with something.

"Where *are* you, Johnny? I ain't gonna hurt you. But your mother's having her baby. She wants you home."

Then the little light coming through the access hole I'd crawled through was blotted out as his head and shoulders filled the opening. He poked inside with a pole of some kind. He backed his head out of the hole and pretty soon a rock came crashing inside. Then another and another. The rocks struck the boiler's sides and end with ear shattering clangs, barely missing me as I made myself as small as I could. I steeled myself to remain silent. Then a rock hit my leg. It hurt something fierce. I bit my upper lip to keep from crying out.

Then I heard him mutter, "Maybe the little bastard ain't in here."

I heard him climb out of the pit and footsteps receding. Once he must have kicked something and it fell with a crash. I stayed where I was until the last glimmer of light faded away and then a while longer. When I scrambled out through the hole the barn was dark, too, only a faint night shine coming through the rear windows and the cracks in the big doors. I felt my way to the back, climbed the post, and clambered out onto the shed roof. Going home I limped slowly, staying in the shadows, fearing at any moment a big, strong hand would seize me. I wondered if my mother was really having the baby. I hoped Dwayne had lied about that, too.

As I entered the back door, my mother came in the kitchen. She stared at me wide-eyed and open-mouthed.

"Great Heavens to Betsy! *Where* have you *been?* You're so dirty I scarcely know it's you."

"I was hiding, Mom."

"Well, you must have picked the filthiest place in town." She looked as though she didn't know whether to swat me or hug me. "Take off those dirty clothes and wash up. Then you can eat your supper."

I just stood there, head down, and thankful to be safe at home.

"I was hiding from Dwayne," I said. "He was after me. He was going to kill me."

She lifted my face and looked with concern into my eyes.

"You *must* be exaggerating," she said. "I *know* he's a wicked young man. But why for heaven's sake would he want to kill you?"

"Remember the day they found Miss Owen in the river?"

My mother nodded.

"Well, Kenneth and me followed Dwayne's car the night before...when he left Miss Owen's place. We followed him to the river below the bluff and saw him dump something into the water. It was so dark we couldn't see exactly what it was. But when they found Miss Owen I got to thinking and I decided maybe it was her body Dwayne had dumped into the river."

"But you couldn't be sure..."

"No. But it's the kind of thing he *would* do if he thought he could get away with it. Mom, you don't know how evil and cruel he can be."

She nodded again and said, "Go on with your story."

"It's not a story, Mom. It's the truth. And I knew it really was the truth when he came up to me this afternoon while I was fishing. He was acting real friendly, but I just hated him and got mad. And I accused him of killing Miss Owen. I told him me and Kenneth saw him push her in the river."

Worry lines were on my mother's face. "Then what happened, Johnny?"

"Well, he had his slingshot so I started running and he started firing rocks at me. He hit me once." I showed her the gash on my arm. "I ran into the willows and got ahead of him and went into the old streetcar barn. That's where I hid...in the tank. He shot rocks into that, too, and hit me bad on my leg." I showed her that wound.

"Mom, he had that crazy look on his face like that day when he burned up a cat."

Her eyes opened in shock. "You never told me about *that*," she said.

"Well, he did it and I know he intended to kill *me* today. And he *will* kill me if he ever catches me."

"Well, we'll just *see* about *that*," she said fiercely. Then she hugged me and cried. She said I should have told her about Dwayne and Miss Owen and about his burning the cat, too. Then she put on her old hat and gloves and walked with me downtown to the police station.

The chief listened intently and looked at my wounds. He said he'd known Dwayne had been hanging around Miss Owen, but he'd had no reason to connect him with anything else. Then he said he would arrest Dwayne that very night. Next morning he came by and told us Dwayne had left town.

Chapter Five   June

    My long awaited summer vacation began with a fearful menace haunting my days and nights. And Kenneth became terrified, too, when I told him what had happened. We stayed close to home, not even venturing to The Logs to fish. Other kids began to swim in the river. But we didn't. Once a day we would sneak cautiously to the police station and ask for news of Dwayne. Every night Kenneth would look through the newspaper and report to me the next morning.
    Dwayne had been seen at a cottage camp in Greybull but when the police went to apprehend him he had disappeared without a trace. Then Dwayne's car was found up in Billings, with a busted wheel bearing, but no sign of the fugitive. Two days later he was arrested in Chugwater, for stealing a car. The newspaper reported he would be returned to our town. Kenneth and I celebrated Dwayne's capture by catching six suckers and trading them to Mrs. Redd for two candy bars and some bones for Paint.
    But our joy was short lived. The next evening's newspaper said Dwayne had overpowered the deputy assigned to bring him back to our county jail and had beaten the man nearly to death. Again he disappeared. Days passed with no further news of him, and we began to hope he had gone clear out of the country...to California or maybe even Mexico...and we'd never see him again.
    No one can stay scared forever, especially boys our age. Except for frequent nightmares—when I'd wake up sweating and breathless, imagining I'd felt big strong fingers choking

me—I began to feel safe during the days. And gradually Kenneth and I took up our summer pursuits.

We swam in the river. We made bows from ash tree branches and arrows from willow shoots and played Robin Hood among the willow and boxelder thickets along the river banks. One day we captured Scrubby, intending to take his money to give to the poor. But he didn't have a cent on him.

We spent part of each day looking in the street gutters and around the saloons down town for Camel cigarette packages. Beneath the glued flap on the bottom of each package were numbers. We'd heard that beneath one flap of every million packages was the word Chevrolet or Ford. Such a package could be exchanged for a new car, so it was said. Every time we peeled off one of those flaps we had high hopes of seeing one of the magic words. But we never found one.

There were a few ways to earn money. Mrs. Graves paid a nickel a bushel for digging dandelions from her lawn. But it took a couple of hours to dig up a bushel, because her lawn didn't have many of the weeds.

Mrs. Bailey gave me a nickel every week for mowing her big lawn. I'd spend more than two hours to push the mower, rake up the clippings and haul them out back of her house. Sometimes she'd give me a dime, but not very often.

And there were still suckers to catch for Mrs. Redd's cats.

My mother looked as if she'd swallowed a pillow. Every now and then she'd have me put my hand on her stomach and I could feel something moving inside. It was kind of spooky to know there was a real baby in there.

One morning after breakfast I carried in a bucket of coal and some kindling. Anna was outside playing with a neighbor girl. Ralph had gone somewhere or other.

My mother said, "It won't be long now until the baby comes."

"Golly," I said. "How do you know?"

"I just know...and I wonder...I'd like to ask you to lend me the rest of your money...to help pay for the baby."

"Gee. How much do they cost, Mom?"

"More than I have. That's how much. The rent is 22 dollars. But I could only pay ten dollars on it this month." She sat on a kitchen chair, her hands under her stomach, and sighed. I hoped she wouldn't cry.

"I still have three dollars and fifty cents after paying for the window, " I said. "Do you think that'll be enough?"

"It will help," she said. "But I hate to ask you. You've been saving so long."

I went to the bedroom, got the money, and took it to her.

"Well, Mom, I'd rather have a new baby around here than a BB gun. What do you think it's gonna be?"

She sighed again. "I hope it's a girl. Then I'll have two of each."

"That'd be really keen. Then she could pester Anna like I pester Ralph."

Just a few nights later I heard her cry out from her bedroom. Ralph got up and dressed and ran to Mrs. Bailey's house. The two of them came back and helped my mother into Mrs. Bailey's car, and they drove off to the hospital. Anna was crying. I felt like it, too, but I didn't because I was older. It was the first time our mother had ever left us alone at night. I told Anna she could come and get in bed with me. Neither of us slept much, though.

At sunrise I got up and built a fire in the kitchen stove. I cut some bread and put it on the stove to toast and tried to remember how my mother made oatmeal. I decided we'd just have toast and milk. About mid-morning Ralph came home. I thought he'd tell us whether it was a boy or a girl. But he said the baby hadn't been born yet. The doctor had told him our mother was having a bad time of it.

Then I remembered once I had overheard my mother talking to Mrs. Chesley, and she said her doctor had told her after Ralph was born she should never have another baby. She told it like it was a joke. She laughed and said, "But I've had two more. And I'm going to have another. It isn't easy for me, but it's worth it." When I remembered that, I started worrying. What if that doctor was right?

We waited all that day, Anna and I, too worried even to fight or pester each other. Ralph stayed at the hospital. He came home and fixed himself some supper and then went back. It was early next morning before he returned. And this time he was smiling.

"We got ourselves a new sister," he said. "But Mom is about beat. We all have to pitch in and help until Grandmother comes."

"How'd she know about it?" I asked.

Ralph kind of stuck out his chest and looked proudly down at Anna and me. "I phoned her," he said, "Long distance. Collect. She'll be here on the train day after tomorrow. I phoned Dad, too. He can't come right away. He said he didn't have enough money to make the trip. But he sure was glad to know Mom is okay...and that Grandmother's coming."

The engine with a string of cars behind came chuffing and puffing, black smoke rising from its stack, up the long flat south of town toward the depot where the three of us waited for Grandmother. The train began to slow, and then came the squealing and shrieking of the engine's steel wheels on steel rails until it stopped alongside the depot and emitted a final whoosh of steam as if to say, "I'm here."

A few passengers clambered down the steps and stretched wearily on the concrete slab in front of the depot. Just as I began to fear Grandmother had missed the train, she came severely down the steps, carrying a small carpetbag and a purse. She gave each of us a peck on the cheek and then told Ralph to fetch a taxi. There was only one in town, but the driver always met the train even though he seldom got a fare.

The taxi stopped in front of our little house and the driver carried Grandmother's large suitcase up to the porch. She paid him and then handed him a coin from the change. I think it was a dime. Then she walked into the house and inspected each room.

We stood awkwardly in the living room until she came back from her tour.

"Do you mean *all* of you live in *this?*" she asked. Then she sighed and said, "Poor Catherine." That was my mother's name. Then she went into the kitchen and started rummaging around in the cupboard.

"We'll need groceries," she called out. "You children are about down to nothing." After a bit, she came out with a piece of paper. "Here's a list of things we need, Ralph. You go and get them." She handed him the list and a bill. It looked like ten dollars. I was impressed.

Ralph read the list. "I'll go across town," he said. "It's cheaper than the little store near us. And when I walk clear over there, Mom always gives me a penny for every nickel I save."

"I don't pay anyone to do his duty," Grandmother said sternly. "Now scoot or we'll have supper for breakfast."

Three days later Grandmother brought our mother and the baby home in the taxi. Anna and I were waiting on the front porch when they arrived. Mom's face was very pale, like she was sick. She held onto Grandmother as she came slowly to the house and greeted us with a wan smile. Behind them Ralph, grinning, carried the baby. Although Mom looked weak and worn out the baby was not. It was bawling loud enough to scare birds out of the trees.

"Her name is Mary," Mom said.

Grandmother said, "Doctor says your mother has to go straight to bed and stay there for at least a week."

A month or so before Mom had borrowed a crib. We had managed to put it beside the bed in her already cramped bedroom by moving the dressing table to the foot of her bed and the chest of drawers into the corner by the door to the living room. There was scarcely enough space to walk between the bed and the crib.

After Mom was put to bed and the baby stopped crying, we all gathered in the kitchen.

Grandmother said, "Your mother will need lots of help. And I will show you how and where to clean...to wash the clothes...and even cook a little. Your new sister's name was my mother's. It's a lovely name if you pronounce it properly. It's May-ree...not Mare-ee. So say it correctly. May-ree."

I nodded, realizing that this was important to her, although I didn't know why. There was a Mary in my classroom and everyone called her Mare-ee.

I was beginning to learn that almost everything had its good points and bad. The good part about having Grandmother with us was that we got to eat things we hadn't had in a long time. Like having chicken on Sunday. Or if not chicken a big beef roast with tasty gravy. Usually pork chops once a week. Bacon and eggs for breakfast. And sometimes ice cream after supper.

The bad part was having to watch my manners and do my chores promptly or get rapped on the head with her thimble which she always had handy in her apron pocket. And then, without fail I had to go to Sunday School and stay over for Church service and even go to prayer meeting on Wednesday nights. It seemed like she only approved of two things: work and worship.

And gol darn but she'd get upset whenever something was temporarily missing. I learned that the first time she asked me to clean up the back yard.

"Where's the rake? You do have a rake, don't you?"

"Yes'm, but I don't know where it is."

"Well, we'll just look for it until we find it."

It took a while but we finally found the rake in some weeds out behind the coal shed. It was very rusty from being there all winter.

"Now, Johnny," she said. "Always remember. A place for everything and everything in its place. The good Lord didn't intend for folks to waste precious time looking for things instead of using them."

When we found the rake she noticed the deep hole Kenneth and I had dug in the vacant lot behind our house. It was about as long and wide as I was tall and over my head deep. Kenneth and I had big plans for that hole. We were going to cover it with planks and have ourselves a cave.

Grandmother said, "Who dug that hole? That's dangerous. Suppose someone fell in there."

"Well," I said, "Kenneth and me dug it so we can have a cave."

She shook her finger at me, and said, "The Lord told Moses 'if a man shall dig a pit...and an ox or ass fall therein; the owner of the pit shall...give money unto the owner of them.' That's from Exodus, in the Bible."

"But Grandmother, there ain't any oxes or asses around here," I said.

"Never you mind," she said. "Suppose a child fell in it and was hurt. That would be worse than if an ox or an ass fell in. Don't argue. I want you to fill in that hole right now. Before supper."

And so I began. It was hard work. I kept thinking how mad Kenneth was going to be when he found our hole filled in. I was late to supper and had to do the dishes, even though it wasn't my turn.

The first Sunday Grandmother gave each of us a nickel for the Sunday School collection. Ralph and Anna went on ahead. I followed slowly behind. Billy Smith, who had got me in trouble more than once before, caught up with me and asked where I was going. I told him and he asked if I had any money. I showed him the nickel. He suggested we stop by Parker's newsstand and look at the magazine covers.

Inside the store I gazed at the lurid illustrations of evil looking men jabbing needles into helpless looking, beautiful ladies or strangling them and the like.

Billy grabbed my sleeve and led me to a door which opened into a small room. In it was a contraption with a row of three windows and a handle on the side.

"It's a slot machine," Billy said. He put a nickel in the slot and pulled the handle. The pictures behind the windows revolved rapidly and came to a stop.

"Yay," Billy exclaimed. "Two cherries!" Three nickels dropped noisily into a cup-like affair on the bottom of the machine. Billy scooped up the nickels and said, "Whyn't you try it?"

"All I've got is my Sunday School money," I said.

"Where do you think I got mine?" he asked. "I come by here every Sunday. I owe the church 70 cents. And I'm gonna pay it back when I hit the jackpot."

Swayed by such a reasonable proposition, I put my nickel in the slot and pulled the handle. Five came clattering out. It was the easiest money I had ever made. I kept putting in nickels and pulling the handle, winning a few but losing more, until I had no nickels left. Then Billy played and lost his three nickels.

Billy said, "Maybe next Sunday I'll hit it. You come with me. With two of us playing we'll get it quicker. And split the money."

We ran the rest of the way to the church and arrived at Sunday school fifteen minutes late. I sat in the back of the room so Ralph and Anna wouldn't see that I didn't put my nickel in the collection. In fact, there was no collection before the hour ended. I felt relieved until later when church was over. Anna told me the teacher had taken the collection before I got there.

"What you gonna do with your nickel?" Anna asked.

"Oh, I'll put it in next week," I said.

"Then you'll have to put in a dime, if Grandmother gives you another one," she said.

During the church service that Sunday, our preacher, the Reverend Mr. Thaddeus T. Rowe, reminded his congregation about the revival meetings that would begin the next evening and continue through Friday night. Grandmother was sitting with my brother and sister in the front row. I was in the back row so's I'd have a head start out of there when the service ended. In fact, I planned to leave a little early because I knew the preacher couldn't see that far.

I'd heard Mrs. Chesley tell my mother that the preacher couldn't see more than twenty feet in front of his nose without his glasses. But he never wore them in church. Mrs. Chesley had said, with a laugh, that he was such a vain man he didn't want to be seen wearing glasses. He thought it made him look old.

So Preacher Rowe squinted down from his pulpit and described the upcoming revival meetings. They would be, he said, an occasion for all saved souls to rejoice in their goodness and for sinners to lament and abandon their evil ways. The meetings would concern the Ten Commandments which God gave to Moses. Two on each of the five nights. And Reverend Rowe had secured the services of a world-renowned evangelist and saver of sinners. I groaned silently, thinking of five summer nights wasted, because I was certain that Grandmother would insist on our attending each meeting.

I was right. Grandmother did intend for us kids to attend all five of the revival meetings. She made arrangements with a neighbor lady to care for our mother and the baby during our absence.

The first night the church was packed with saints and sinners. But we had arrived early and Grandmother made me sit in front with her, Anna and Ralph. Our preacher introduced the Reverend Mr. Matthew Paul Simmons who, Reverend Rowe said—his eyes squinting heavenwards—had saved many a thousand sinners in every corner of the globe.

Beside the pulpit was a table stacked with a matched set of dinnerware: shiny new china bowls, saucers, plates, and cups. Reverend Simmons began praying, and continued on and on, with thanks for the congregation's saved souls and pleas for redemption of the sinners. I closed my eyes and fell asleep and was jolted awake by a sharp poke from Grandmother's elbow. The praying had stopped and the main course began.

The evangelist thrust his right arm upward, forefinger pointing heavenwards, while he thundered out the words God gave to Moses: "Thou shalt have no other gods before me." He paused and then nodded at preacher Rowe, who seized one of the plates and struck it with a little hammer. The broken pieces clattered to the floor. Reverend Simmons thundered on and on about the dreadful punishment awaiting anyone so bold or foolish as to put God in second place.

At length, when the idea of having other gods was thoroughly discredited, Reverend Simmons turned his oratory onto the second commandment. "Thou shalt not make unto thee any graven image." And he shouted and carried on even more fiercely than before about the graven images, which I gathered included anything in the sky, the earth, or the water. And every time he said "Thou shalt not" our preacher would grab another dish and smash it with his hammer. In his zeal, Reverend Simmons would leave the pulpit from time to time and stalk about, the broken china crackling beneath his feet.

I was wide awake now. I'd never seen such a to-do before, in church or out. I thought of the new china dishes being broken and then of the mismatched, chipped and cracked ones we had at home. I was fascinated by the spectacle but saddened at the waste.

After more than an hour of the thundering and shouting and breaking of dishes, Reverend Simmons was red-faced and sweating as though he actually had been wrestling with the Devil, whom he mentioned frequently. He sat down beside the pulpit and fanned himself while the collection was taken. After the final prayer, I asked Grandmother if I could go up and talk to him. She smiled her approval and nudged me forward.

I approached the preacher and he took my hand but didn't stand up.

"And what can I do for you, my little man," he said and wiped sweat from his face.

"Well, sir," I said. "I was thinking about those dishes."

"That will make you think very hard indeed about not breaking the Lord's commandments. Won't it?"

"Yes, sir. But I was wondering if I could bring down some of our old dishes from home and trade you for the new ones...before you break them. Our dishes are cracked and don't match. And it wouldn't be much loss if you broke them. I'd even trade you two for one."

He dropped my hand and glared at me. "I don't think you got the point, boy," he said. "That simply wouldn't do. When you break one of the Lord's commandments, it's the same as breaking a new, unblemished, perfect dish. No. We couldn't use your old cracked dishes at all." He stood up and stalked away. I could tell he was mad.

Grandmother patted me on the head, and said, "It was nice of you to go up and talk to the preacher. Didn't he just make you think?"

"Yes'm," I said, thinking about the broken dishes and how my mother would like to have them.

The next night the evangelist started off with "Thou shalt not take the name of thy Lord in vain." If anything, he fussed and fumed more furiously than the night before, and our preacher broke even more dishes. It appeared to me that cursing was even worse than making images. Even saying "gosh" or "gol" was blackest sin, he said, because those words were only a coverup, a sneaky way to take the Lord's name in vain. And the Lord would not be fooled nor forgive such breaking of his law.

And so it went, night after night, as Reverend Simmons raged and stormed about the thou-shalts and thou-shalt-nots and hell and the Devil...two commandments at each evening's meeting. On Thursday night he took up 'Thou shalt not steal.' And he aimed that one right at me and Billy, or so I imagined.

After having Preacher Rowe break a few dishes, the evangelist said, "I tell you, brothers and sisters...and especially you young people...there's scarcely no sin worse than stealing. It can start with sneaking some jam from your mother's cupboard. And then one day you'll steal some money. And then you'll rob a bank and wind up in prison. But that's *nothing* compared to the punishment the Lord gives for breaking his commandment against stealing. Did you ever burn yourself on a hot stove? Remember how it hurt? If you steal, you will spend *all* eternity roasting in the *fiery* furnace of *hell*. Just think of it children—and especially you boys—confined night and day...*forever*...in the *fiery*...*furnace*...of *hell*."

"No," the preacher went on, "boys and girls are not apt to make graven images...or commit adultery. But they *are* tempted to steal. And I tell you stealing is the sin that starts *all* the others...starts you on the road to *all* the other sins the Lord has forbade you to commit...because he loves you...and will *punish* you if you disobey Him."

I thought about the nickel I'd put in the slot machine. It didn't seem fair that would doom me to eternity in hell's fiery furnace. But I resolved to pay it back next time I had a nickel, just in case the preacher was right.

Each day I had been telling Kenneth about the big show at church. He was a Catholic and told me about the goings on in his church...how they burned incense and sprinkled water around and prayed in a language Kenneth didn't understand.

On Thursday I asked Grandmother if I could invite Kenneth to go with us on Friday and she agreed. That last night was not as dramatic as some of the others. The subjects were about bearing false witness and coveting thy neighbor's house or wife or anything else he had. I think Reverend Simmons was getting tired. He didn't carry on as vigorously as earlier in the week. But there were still lots of dishes to break, and before the revival ended that night, Preacher Rowe had smashed every last one.

When we left the church, I asked Grandmother if I could go by Kenneth's house to see Paint. She said all right if I'd stay only a little while. What we really intended to do was go by Parker's newsstand and look at the pulp magazine covers. I'd told Kenneth that the latest batch were the scariest ever, and he was eager to see them.

Mr. Parker was alone inside the newsstand. He rose from a chair at the rear of the store as we entered and then sat down again when we walked over to the magazine display. I guess he was used to kids coming in to look at the magazines but never buying one.

"Oh, my gosh, look at this one," Kenneth said, "...look at that werewolf biting that pretty lady. See the blood running down her neck?"

"Golly," I exclaimed. "Look at this vampire coming out of a coffin. Look at those teeth. Whoever he bites will turn into a vampire, too."

We moseyed along the display rack, staring at scenes of stabbings, shootings, violence, and horrors of every description. I pointed to one titled *Terror of Fu Manchu*. A wispy bearded man with evil eyes was poking a needle into the arm of a wide-eyed, terrified, sparsely clad blonde lady.

I said, "Those eyes make me think of Dwayne when he's mad. Like that day he chased me after he killed Miss Owen."

"Yeah," Kenneth said solemnly. "Let's get out of here. I've seen enough."

Upon leaving the newsstand both of us were thoroughly frightened. And to make matters worse we began talking about Dwayne...wondering where he was...whether he would ever come back...and what we'd do if he did return. We agreed that wherever he was Dwayne was thinking about getting even with us.

Not a soul was in sight on Main Street, adding to our fear. We had almost reached the corner of the side street which led toward our homes when we saw old Louie come out of a saloon and stagger into the street. He was the town's most confirmed drunkard. Mrs. Redd wouldn't even let him stay in one of her shacks. If he had a last name I'd never known it. He was just old Louie, the drunk.

He'd almost reached the middle of the street when a car came zooming around the corner, and continued without pause right toward Louie. Kenneth and I yelled. But the car struck Louie and sent him flying. The car screeched to a stop. The driver scrambled out and peered toward the body lying in the street.

"Lookee, there, Kenneth," I said. "That's our preacher. See, he's taking something from his pocket. He's putting on his *glasses*! Gollee! He can't even see the back of the church without them. No wonder he ran over old Louie."

By this time several men had come out of the saloon and from another one just up the street. They gathered around Louie, who began to move and then sat up and stared at the faces above him.

Preacher Rowe was waving his arms and talking excitedly. I heard him say, "He just jumped right in front of my car."

One of the bystanders said, "The old drunk shouldn't have been out in the street anyways."

At my side, Kenneth said, "Seems to me there ought to be one more commandment."

"What for?" I asked.

"Thou shalt not drive without your glasses if you can't see the back of your church or a man in the middle of the street."

"Amen," I said, with a laugh. Then we took off running for our homes.

By the end of the third week my mother was almost her old self, cooking and singing and, of course, spending lots of time caring for the baby. Ralph and I had been sleeping on the floor in the living room so that Grandmother could have our bed.

One day she went over to Mrs. Bailey's and phoned for the taxi to take her to the train station. We kids rode with her and waved goodbye from the platform. Then we walked home. I knew I would miss her. But I was glad she had gone, too, glad our house was back to the way it had been. Except now we had a baby to play with.

Several days later Kenneth and I took sandwiches and hiked up beyond the bluff to a marshy place between sandy hills called Dead Man's Gulch. It was called that, folks said, because a man had been murdered there a long time ago. It *was* kind of a spooky place. Only the cries of redwing blackbirds and whispers of the wind broke the silence.

We liked to go there, because the area was home to all kinds of wildlife...frogs, snakes, birds, rabbits and what not. We had our slingshots in hopes of shooting a rabbit. We saw one just as we began to descend a hill toward the marsh. But we both missed it. Paint chased that rabbit until they both were almost out of sight before he decided he couldn't catch it and came panting back.

Kenneth and I each had a cloth sugar sack because we hoped to find some good specimens for the animal show we planned to stage, someday. We also had a quart jar to put frog eggs in. Just a ways short of the marshy area we came across the strangest creature we'd ever seen. It was greyish-tan in color, about the size of my hand and scurried along on short little legs, its belly scraping the ground. Sharp little horn-like projections adorned its head. We feared to touch it but with the aid of sticks we finally chased it into one of the sugar sacks.

"I bet that'll be the star of the show," Kenneth said.

"Yeah. Whatever it is."

Nearer the marsh we scared up a snake, about three feet long. At first I thought it was a rattlesnake. But it didn't make that buzzing noise. We headed it off from the marsh and finally pinned it down with our sticks.

"That's a king snake," I said. "Dr. Hammond told me about them. They look a lot like rattlers. But see, it hasn't any rattles on its tail. Dr. Hammond says king snakes *eat* rattle snakes, but they won't hurt people. It'll be great for our animal show." I grabbed its tail and plopped it into my sugar sack.

We went on down to the marsh and hunted around until we found a cluster of frog eggs. We put them in water inside our jar. When the eggs hatched into tadpoles, with their fat little bodies and a tail behind, we figured they would be a great attraction for our animal show.

Just then we heard Paint barking excitedly from a thicket across the marsh. Then came a howl of pain and Paint streaked out, shaking his head as though a swarm of bees was attacking him, then stopping and scraping at his face with his front paws. All the while he kept on yelping and whimpering.

We crossed the marsh by hopping from one dry hummock to another. When we reached Paint we saw porcupine quills all over his muzzle. We peered into the thicket and saw the bristly animal, its back turned to us, its tail full of quills raised. Paint made a move to attack the spiny creature again, but Kenneth and I each grabbed one of the dog's hind legs and held on while the porcupine ambled slowly away until it was out of sight in the thicket.

Paint kept pawing at his face, breaking some quills off until only stubs could be seen and pushing others deeper into his flesh.

I said, "I believe he was gonna take after that porky again."

"He's a slow learner," Kenneth said. "What're we gonna do? He's really hurting."

"We gotta try to get those quills out. They'll keep moving in until they puncture his eyes or maybe his brain."

Paint was lying down now, only occasionally pawing at his face. He seemed to have learned that it only made the hurt worse. We tried to pull out some of the quills. But Paint would jerk his head around and then get up and move away.

"I got an idea," I said. "If we dig a pit in this sand and cover him up, may be he won't be able to move and we can get some of the quills out."

With our hands we scooped a big hole in the sand and coaxed Paint into lying in it. Then we pushed sand on top of him until only his head was uncovered. Then we tried again to pull out some of the quills. But he was so strong that even with all that sand on him he was able to struggle out and move away, eyeing us suspiciously. We covered him again, but he just wouldn't lie there and let us pull out those quills.

"Well," I said, "I think we gotta take him to Dr. Hammond. He'll know what to do."

So we made haste back toward town, Paint plodding along behind and whimpering every now and then.

Luckily Dr Hammond was in his office. He looked at Paint and whistled. He said, "I never saw such a snootful of porcupine quills. Most dogs back off with just a few. He must have hit that porky more than once. That dog has more guts than sense."

"Can you get the quills out?" I asked. Then I told him how we had tried to do it, and he laughed.

"I'll just put him to sleep and then I'll pull the quills with these forceps." He showed us the scissors-like instrument with jaws like pliers.

Half an hour later he'd pulled out the quills and Paint was beginning to wake up. He was pretty groggy, not nearly so frisky as before he'd tangled with the porcupine.

"Golly, thanks, Dr. Hammond," I said. "How much do we owe you?" He pursed his lips, thought for a moment and then said, "Well, for a job like that, I usually charge five dollars."

I looked at Kenneth and knew he was as staggered as I was at running up such a huge debt.

To our relief Dr. Hammond said, "We won't talk about that now. Let's just say you boys owe me. And maybe someday we can figure out a way for you to pay me back."

Then we showed him our trophies.

"Yup," he said. "That's a king snake all right. And the other little fellow is a horned toad. There aren't many of them in this country. But they're fairly common in the desert down south."

Chapter Six   July

During the two weeks before the Fourth of July Kenneth and I worked harder than ever before to earn money for fireworks. We scoured Mrs. Graves' huge lawn for an entire afternoon and dug up two bushels of dandelions. She reminded us frequently to put every worm that came up with the roots back into the ground. After complaining that the bushel baskets weren't quite full, she paid us ten cents for our work.

I mowed Mrs. Bailey's big lawn twice including an extra good job one time, clipping along all the borders and the sidewalk. She gave me a dime for that and a nickel for the other time. Kenneth did some extra work for his mother and she paid him a dime.

We scoured the town over for beer and pop bottles and looked for them alongside the highway at each end of town. We managed to find thirteen. Paint had learned about our interest in bottles and he often discovered one out of sight where we'd never have found it. He'd grab it in his mouth and bring it proudly to us.

Then we heard the city would hire twenty boys to clear weeds out of the cemetery on the Saturday before the Fourth. Kenneth and I went out there extra early so's we'd be sure to get jobs. And we worked all day, hacking off weeds with hoes and shovels, raking the weeds into piles, choking on dust and sweating in the hot sun. When the job was finished at day's end, the palms of our hands were red and blistered. We collected our pay, 50 cents apiece, but were so tired we just barely made it home.

We then had over a dollar between us, enough to celebrate Independence Day in a big way. We bought firecrackers, cherry bombs, and torpedoes, which exploded on impact. The rockets and roman candles were too expensive. Besides, we wanted fireworks that made a lot of noise.

We each bought a cap pistol; not one of the usual kind that used rolls of caps, but a new kind of pistol that was loaded with disks of six caps that revolved and fired just like a real western six gun. We had great fun playing cowboy. We took turns being Tom Mix, the greatest of the movie cowboys. Buck Jones was second best. Hoot Gibson, Hopalong Cassidy, Tim McCoy and Roy Rogers were much farther down our scale of cowboy heroes.

The morning of the Fourth came, bright and sunny. From near and far I could hear the explosions. Kenneth and I met out behind our shed and fired off a number of our wares. Paint cowered and whimpered each time we shot one off. He'd run off a ways and then come back. Finally he disappeared altogether. Before long my mother came out and told us to go somewhere else. She said it was time for baby Mary's morning nap and she wouldn't sleep with all that noise.

So Kenneth and I went over to Main Street and found a good place to sit on the curb and watch the parade. After a while we heard the high school band playing, and the parade was underway. First came the mayor riding in a new Buick convertible and waving to folks on both sides of the street. Then the American Legion drum and bugle corps and ranks of veterans of World War I marched by and behind them some older men, veterans of the Spanish American war.

The parade went on...the high school band almost drowning out a barbershop quartet...the county's mounted posse of horsemen...new cars and tractors adorned with the dealers' names...a few Indians from the reservation north of town. Then came the Shriners with their funny hats, throwing out pieces of candy. Kenneth and I managed to grab a few. And last came the National Guard cavalry troop which my father had commanded before he went to South Dakota. Someone else was riding his horse. That reminded me how much I missed my father.

The parade over, Kenneth and I made our way through the crowd and back to our neighborhood where we shot off the rest of our fireworks. We would light a firecracker and put a can over it and when it exploded the can would fly up. Then one of us would put a cherry bomb in a slingshot, draw back on the patch while the other lit the fuse, then let 'er fly. The bomb would sail away and burst in the air.

That night there was a band concert and the two of us had a great time. We had a dime left so we bought two bottles of pop. We played tag with a gang of the neighborhood kids and came across a couple smooching in a dark place.

"That reminds me of old Dwayne," I whispered to Kenneth.

"Yeah, I almost wish he was still around so we could go up on the bluff and bang on his tires."

"Oh, Lordee, don't say that, Kenneth. You gotta be careful what you wish because you might get it. If Dwayne was here, we'd likely be floating in the river like Miss Owen."

Paint didn't show up again for two days when all the fireworks noise was over. We had worried that he wouldn't come back in time for our animal show. Dr. Hammond had agreed we could use his barn for the event.

Our collection was impressive. Miss Gilmore, the baby pigeon I'd taken from the old streetcar barn, would be a prehistoric bird, before they learned to fly. Because Miss Gilmore *didn't*. She was a strange looking pigeon. She had scarcely any feathers on her body. She had wing and tail feathers, but somehow seemed to prefer hopping along on the ground to flying. I had to put her in the coal shed every night so the cats wouldn't catch her.

And Miss Gilmore had never learned to coo like a grown pigeon, but only cheeped like a baby chick. Dr. Hammond told me that might be because she had never been around other pigeons, and her lack of feathers might be due to her diet. When I first brought her home from the streetcar barn the only food I could get down her throat was bread soaked in milk. And she had never developed a taste for anything else. You never saw her picking up seeds, grain, and sand like other pigeons. She'd just hop to the back door and cheep away until I brought her some bread and milk.

Paint would be a great white wolf. A neighbor had a striped alley cat we planned to borrow. We had the horned toad, the king snake, an owl with a sprained wing that hissed ferociously whenever anyone came near it, a quart jar containing half a dozen wasps. And the frog eggs had hatched into tadpoles which swam in water inside a gallon vinegar jar. Little legs had begun to form on their fat bodies. They'd be frogs before much longer.

The day arrived for the big animal show. We'd hand printed notices and tacked them up on telephone poles around the neighborhood. We'd talked up the show to every kid we met. We expected a big turnout.

Early that morning we captured Mrs. Miller's striped alley cat. It was not a very happy cat when we crammed it into a cardboard box for transport to the barn. But an hour and a few scratches later we had the cat inside a wooden apple box with chicken wire on the open side. It looked grand. Whenever we came close to the box the cat would raise its back and bare its little teeth. We hoped it would stay in that mood until the show was over.

At showtime, 10 o'clock, over two dozen kids were lined up at the barn door. Kenneth collected the admission price as they entered: fifteen pins for one kid or a penny would admit two. I looked out and there was Gwendolyn Chesley. She held up a penny and pointed to her little brother. When all the kids were inside, I got up on a platform we'd built from some of Dr. Hammond's lumber.

"Ladies and gentlemen," I hollered, in imitation of a carnival barker I'd heard once. "Welcome to the greatest animal show ever in these parts."

The kids faced me in the space between the various displays and I continued. "We're gonna tell you about all these rare creatures in just a moment. But first I want to show you an animal that doesn't have to be in a cage, because he's so well behaved." I paused for effect and then announced, "...the great white wolf from up in the land where it's always snow and ice the year 'round."

I snapped my fingers and whistled and Paint came bounding up onto the platform.

The audience gazed in silence but Billy Smith shouted, "Aw, that's only old Paint. He ain't no white wolf."

"Yes," I retorted, "*you* know him as old Paint who wouldn't hurt a chickadee. That's because me and Kenneth have tamed him. But he's really a great white wolf that can lick a polar bear."

I snapped my fingers again and Kenneth, who was out of sight behind the platform, played a single, high note on his harmonica. Paint raised his nose toward the roof and howled. Again, Kenneth played the note and again Paint howled and then howled again. He always did that whenever Kenneth played the harmonica.

"If that ain't the cry of a great white wolf, I'll..." I almost said they could have their money back, but I feared that they might take it.

"Now," I went on in my carnival barker's voice, "I will tell you about our other attractions.

"Starting up front on your left is the only baby dinosaur around that I know of." They gathered around a dishpan in which we'd placed the horned toad, pushing and shoving to get in front where they could see.

"Give me your attention, ladies and gentlemen, and I'll tell you about the other exhibits and then Kenneth and I will answer any questions you have.

"Next to the baby dinosaur is a rare collection of killer wasps from Africa. They say one sting will kill you. But don't worry. These are safe inside that jar."

I pointed to a ten-gallon pickle crock on top of another apple box. "Inside that crock is one of the deadliest snakes in the world...from the jungles of the Amazon River...more deadly than a rattlesnake by far.

"And then you'll see practically the only prehistoric bird in existence...before they learned to grow feathers all over and fly." Miss Gilmore was in an open topped cardboard box, trotting around and cheeping.

I talked about the owl that hissed and lastly I introduced "...a baby tiger from India. Be careful you don't stick your fingers in the cage. He might bite them right off."

By this time our audience was walking around from one exhibit to another. So I jumped down from the platform with Paint at my heels. I reached the cage containing the baby tiger just in time to hear Billy Smith say, "Aw, that's only Mrs. Miller's cat. This show is a big fake."

Beside me Paint put his nose up against the chicken wire and sniffed. Fast as lightning the cat struck with one front paw, its claws piercing the dog's nose. Paint yelped and pulled back. Then he growled deep in his throat and leaped for the cage. The chicken wire came off as the box fell back. The cat streaked away with Paint hot after it, knocking over the crock which contained our snake.

The snake slithered out of the crock and Gwendolyn screamed. Then the other kids starting yelling and running to escape the snake, knocking over our exhibits one after the other. I scooped up Miss Gilmore so she wouldn't get stepped on. The tadpoles lay flopping in the dirt. The owl hopped away, somehow avoiding the pounding feet. The wasp jar fell and broke. The angry insects stung Billy Smith and Gwendolyn's little brother. Their cries of pain added to the pandemonium as every kid tried to be first out the barn door.

When only Kenneth and I were left inside the barn, we looked at each other and began laughing.

"That's *one* show they'll never forget," Kenneth said.

"And we won't either," I said. "I'm glad Billy got stung. Serves him right for trying to ruin our show. By the way, how much did we take in?"

"Not very much. Nine cents and 255 pins."

"Only *nine* cents?" I groaned. "What're we gonna do with all those pins?"

"Give 'em to our mothers, I guess. Those kids' mothers are gonna be wonderin' what happened to *their* pins."

"I bet we'd have made more money if we let 'em in three for a penny," I said.

"Yeah. Well, we can try that next year."

That afternoon we rode over to Mrs. Redd's store. The bell jingled and when she saw us she put on a big smile.

"Where've you boys been? I been savin' you a big surprise."

"We've been awful busy with Fourth of July and our animal show," I said. "What's the surprise?"

She reached behind and brought the box of chocolate mints onto the counter. We'd never won anything since the first time when Kenneth got a red center and won a yo-yo.

Mrs. Redd tipped the box so we could see inside. "There's only ten mints left," she said, "And there's still one yo-yo and the pocketknife to be won. Take all ten of the mints and you get the prizes for sure. I been savin' these for you because you boys is such good customers. I thought you'd bring me five or six suckers and that'd take the whole kaboodle."

"We haven't been fishin' much what with the Fourth and our show," I said.

"We'll go fishing tomorrow, Mrs. Redd." Kenneth said. "Can you hold them until then?"

"Well, I keep thinking someone will come in and ask to take a chance. And if they do, I'd have to let 'em. And likely they'd take them all. Business is business, you know."

Kenneth and I left the counter and whispered to each other for a bit. Then we went back and counted the mints in the box...just ten left.

Kenneth nudged me and I said, "We have nine cents, Mrs. Redd. Couldn't you let us have all ten of them for that?" I gave her my most pleading look.

She hesitated for a moment and then said, "No, I reckon I can't do that. Business is business, you know."

Kenneth begged, "Well, how about we owe you a penny? We'll catch a couple of suckers this afternoon and pay you back."

"I never allow any credit, boys. That's how I stay in business." She appeared to be thinking, then she said, "Whyn't you just pick nine? You got nine chances out of ten to win.

And likely you'll win the yo-yo and the knife before you pick even four or five."

Kenneth and I conferred again and decided she was probably right. So one at a time we took turns picking mints from the box. On the fourth pick I got a red center and won the yo-yo. We continued picking mints, one by one, expecting each one would have a green center and we'd win the jackknife.

We could scarcely believe our eyes when Kenneth broke open the ninth mint and revealed a *white* center. We looked at the last mint in the box. There it was. The one with a green center. And we had no more money.

It was very quiet inside Mrs. Redd's store. She seemed as disappointed as we were.

"Boys!" she exclaimed. "I just can't believe it. I wanted you to win that knife."

"I got an idea," Kenneth said. "Mrs. Redd, we have 265 pins we collected at our show. I have 'em right here in a little box. That many pins must be worth at least a penny."

"What would I do with so many loose pins? The ladies who buy pins here buy those little packages, with the pins all in a row stuck through the pages." She stopped talking and seemed to be thinking again. "No, I guess I couldn't do that. It's not good business."

We turned sadly away and began walking toward the door, when Mrs. Redd spoke again. "Oh, pshaw," she said. "Give me the pins and take the knife."

Kenneth handed her the box of pins. Then each of us took hold of one side of the last mint and broke it in two and gaped at it. It had a *white* center! We couldn't believe our eyes.

Mrs. Redd said, "If that don't beat all. Whatever happened to that green center?"

"Well, who gets the pocket knife?" I asked.

"I don't know," she said. She seemed genuinely confused. "I'll have to think about that. The knife is supposed to go to the person who gets a green center."

Kenneth and I started walking toward the door. We had opened it when Mrs. Redd called out. "Just a minute, boys. I got it figgered out."

We returned to the candy counter.

Mrs. Redd beamed. "What I'm gonna do...is pretend that last mint had a green center...and you boys won the grand prize." She held out the knife. "And take them pins with you, too. When you catch one, bring me a sucker for my cats."

We left the store talking about how one of us would keep the knife for a week and then the other for a week.

Chapter Seven   August

Early one afternoon Kenneth, Paint and I were wandering along a street looking for Camel cigarette packages for want of anything better to do.

Kenneth said, "If I ever find a lucky one, I hope it says Ford on it."

"I'd rather have a new Chevy," I said.

"Not me. Fords have a V-8 engine and hydraulic brakes. A man down at Brown's Motors told me that's why Fords are better than Chevies."

"Yeah, but Chevrolets have that no-draft ventilation and they're more dependable. I guess I oughta know. My Dad drives a car every day in his business, and he says Chevies are the best. Your dad hardly ever drives a car."

We'd had this argument so many times we knew it by heart. But it was too hot to continue on for hours as we usually did.

"How about going swimming?" I suggested.

"Nah. Maybe tomorrow," Kenneth said. We walked slowly along looking for cigarette packages and bottles. Then Kenneth broke the silence.

"Have you ever been drunk, Johnny?"

"No. I never have. Why?"

"My father gets drunk all the time. He's jolly and happy when he starts. Then he gets mean and hits my mom. And hits me, too...if he catches me."

"Kenneth, my mother would skin me alive if she ever caught me drinking. I smoked a cigarette once. I didn't like it. But Ralph and me smoke corn silk and coffee grounds sometimes. They make a lot of smoke and don't taste so terrible and make me cough like tobacco does."

We walked on for a while, then Kenneth said, "I got an idea. Let's go down the alleys behind the saloons...and we'll collect what's left in the empty bottles...until we get enough to taste it."

And so we did. From trash cans behind the saloons on both sides of Main Street we extracted emptied bottles and drained what was left of their contents into one bottle——a few drops from some of the empties and a teaspoon or more from others.

Once Kenneth said, "Golly, look at this pink stuff. The label says 'Sloe Gin.' I wish we'd find more of that. It looks good."

"Yeah. So does that Port wine...and that white stuff that smells like peppermint. But mostly we're only finding whiskey. It don't look good and it smells terrible."

By mid afternoon we had rummaged through the trash can behind the last saloon. Our collecting bottle was almost half full. We found a paper sack and put the bottle in it. Then we started off to our hideout behind Dr. Hammond's house.

"Well, who's gonna try 'er first?" Kenneth asked, from his perch on a stack of lumber.

"You go ahead," I said. "It was your idea."

Kenneth took a little sip and then he shuddered and shook his head.

"It tastes awful," he said. "Now it's your turn."

So I took a sip. It felt as though I'd swallowed fire, from my throat down into my stomach.

"Not bad," I said casually, as I imagined Yancey Cravat would have said in *Cimmaron*. "I've tasted worse."

"Maybe she just takes a little gettin' used to," Kenneth said. "Let me try 'er again." He took a big swallow. His eyes bugged out and he choked and spluttered and yelled out, "Yahoo!"

"Be quiet, Kenneth. Do you want Dr. Hammond to come out and find us with this stuff?"

I took another swig from the bottle and added more fire to that already in my throat and stomach.

Kenneth started giggling and I did, too. Kenneth slapped his hand on his thigh and said, "It sure tastes bad, but it makes me feel funny."

We kept on taking little swigs and then bigger ones and laughing. Whatever we said struck us as the funniest remark ever. We even laughed at the way Paint was looking at us, his head cocked first on one side then the other with that puzzled look he always had when he tried to figure out some new game we were playing.

When the bottle was empty we tried walking clumsily around and then flopped down on a stack of boards. I stretched out on my back and closed my eyes. It felt like the whole world was whirling around so I opened my eyes. That helped stop the gyrations. I didn't feel anything was funny any more. I felt sick. Then I sat up quickly and threw up...again and again until it felt like my stomach was trying to come out of my mouth. Kenneth was doing the same. We looked at each other, got unsteadily to our feet and started off to our homes.

I went in the back way, crawled through the open bedroom window, and dropped onto the bed. I couldn't close my eyes because when I did the sickening, whirling feeling would begin again.

Then I heard my mother call from the living room. "Is that you, Johnny? Come here. I want to show you what Mary can do. She's learned to patty cake."

I groaned and stayed on the bed. Then I heard her steps coming down the hall and into the bedroom. She had baby

Mary in her arms. The baby was smiling and throwing her arms around and jabbering.

My mother said, "What's wrong with you? You look sick."

"Oh, Mom, I *am*. Just let me stay here in bed for a while."

She bent over and felt my forehead. "You don't seem to have a fever. Whatever in the world..."

Then she straightened up, looked sternly down at me and said, "What's that odor?" She bent over and sniffed at my face. "*Johnny!* Have *you* been *drinking?*"

I nodded. Then I told her about it. When I finished, she said, "Well...my good gracious sakes alive. What *am* I going to do with you?"

"Mom, that was the terriblest stuff I ever drank. It was even terribler than castor oil. And, Mom, when I get well I'm gonna sign that card at the church...and promise never, ever, to drink that stuff again in my life."

I felt okay the next day. But for punishment I wasn't allowed to leave our yard for a whole week. The only place I was allowed to go was the Andrew Carnegie Public Library, providing I came right back home.

Since my twelfth birthday in April the librarian had allowed me to check out books from the adult section. I could take six books at a time. I had started by browsing through the books until I found one that looked exciting. Then if it was a good one I'd read others by the same author. I began reading everything I could find on the shelves by Edgar Rice Burroughs, Alexandre Dumas, Rider S. Haggard, Jack London, Rafael Sabatini, James Willard Schultz, and P. C. Wren. I loved their tales of heroes, villains, and adventure.

Usually I read only two books a week because I was too busy playing with Paint and Kenneth. But during my week of confinement I hadn't much to do except read—two or three books a day. My mother kept saying it wasn't much punishment to have time to read so many books. She gave me a few extra chores to do, but I know she really didn't mind my reading. She preferred that to the scrapes I was always getting into.

One day from inside our house I saw the mailman come onto the front porch and heard him raise the flap of the tin mailbox and then leave. I went to the box and found a letter from my father. I took it to the kitchen and handed it to my mother. She sat down right away, opened the envelope and read the letter without a word. Then she looked at me and laughed and then hugged me.

"Your father's coming home...to see his new baby girl and you kids and me."

"Oh, boy," I exclaimed. "That's really keen. Sometimes I almost forget what he looks like. Is he gonna stay for good?"

"No. Just a few days. He has to go back to his job." She read the letter again, a big smile on her face. "He'll get here late Friday afternoon."

All that week I thought about things I wanted to tell my father...about Dwayne's trying to kill me. And I'd ask him to tell me why Chevies were better than Fords for my arguments with Kenneth about which was the better car. Of course, I wanted my father to see Paint and tell him about all the fish I had caught that summer.

On Friday Ralph, Anna, and I cleaned the house with a minimum of arguing over who was working the hardest. Mom managed to scrape up enough money to buy a pot roast and had it on the stove cooking when I heard a car stop out in front of the house. I guess everyone else heard it, too, because we were all standing on the porch when my father climbed the steps carrying his suitcase.

He kissed my mother then he stepped back and stared at her. She was wearing the old dress she wore every day around the house. It was clean but frayed and mended and patched in a couple of places.

"My God!" he exclaimed. "Don't you have anything better than that to wear?"

"Yes," she said to him. "But this is what I wear around the house. There isn't much money for clothes."

My father kind of choked, like a sob. He reached out and grabbed the front of my mother's dress and ripped it away from her body. She stood there for a moment, her dress in tatters, and then ran crying to their little bedroom.

He looked around at us, a wild expression on his face. "This damn depression..." he muttered, "it doesn't leave a man *anything*." Then he stormed out of the house and walked away towards Main Street.

I could hear my mother sobbing in the bedroom. After a while I went in. She was lying curled up, in her torn dress. Baby Mary was lying on her back, cooing, and playing with her feet. My mother turned and sat on the bed, wiping tears from her eyes. She tried to smile.

I said, "Why did you wear that old dress, Mom? When you knew he was coming home? You have a nicer one you wore when you used to go to church."

She began to sob again. "I don't know. I thought I'd have time to change." She paused and looked at me. "No. That's not true. I guess I wanted him to see how things are with us. Him driving around in a car. Living in hotels. Even if they *are* cheap ones. Eating in cafes, while I...we...no, Johnny, I don't mean that about your father. He's a *good* man. He does the best he can. And he loves us. I know. It's just that sometimes I *don't* know what's to become of us. It's these times. I just can't think straight anymore. I wonder if we can cope."

Then she smiled and reached out and took my hand. "Your father loves us. And I love him." She paused again, thinking. "There now. I've said too much. You needn't worry. We're going to make it. I hate quitters. And we're not going to quit...your father, or me, or any of us."

She wiped her eyes and smiled again. "I'll put on my good dress and finish cooking."

A short time later my father returned. His eyes were red as if he might have been crying, too. He went right to the kitchen where my mother was, wearing her good dress. He kissed her and held her for a long time. Then he turned to the three of us where we stood in the doorway.

"I've never been good at apologizing," he said. "But I want each of you to know I'm sorry for what I did. You are all good soldiers. Your mother, too. And I love each of you...very much."

He hugged Anna and me and shook Ralph's hand. Then he went in and picked up baby Mary. He smiled and laughed and talked baby talk and said she was the prettiest girl he'd seen since Anna was born.

His three days passed quickly. He became very angry when I told him about Dwayne. He said he wished he could get his hands on Dwayne and assured me the law would soon catch the fugitive. I learned a lot of good arguments for Chevies from him. He praised old Paint when I brought the dog over to see him every day. He said Paint should be in the movies like that other dog. He said he was proud of me for catching so many fish.

He had long talks with Ralph. And each evening he read to Anna and me from his Collier's magazine. It was mostly about the New Deal and Roosevelt and stuff like that. I didn't understand much of it nor did Anna, I'm sure. But it was pleasant to hear his voice and I knew I would miss him more than ever when he left again.

At breakfast the morning he had to leave, he said he had almost sold an electric light plant in South Dakota...if only the rancher could borrow the money to pay for it. And if the sale went through, he would send us a hundred dollars. I couldn't imagine so much money all at once.

He looked at my mother and joked, "Maybe you can manage to buy a few new dresses."

She said, "And for you some new shoes."

Just before he left the house, my father and mother kissed and then clung to each other for quite a while. I think there were tears in both their eyes.

One morning near the end of the month Kenneth came over to my house and told me that Paint had disappeared.

He said, "I whistled and whistled. I yelled and yelled. But he didn't show up. Remember? He ran away on the Fourth and didn't come home 'til the next day."

"That was because he couldn't stand all that noise," I said.

"I know. But we haven't even shot our cap pistols for quite a while."

"It's mighty strange. Let's go look for him. You know, someone's been poisoning dogs. Two got killed just this week."

"Golly, who'd want to poison Paint? He don't bother anybody."

"Well, Kenneth, people who poison dogs just throw out poisoned meat and don't care which dog eats it."

"It's the sort of thing old Dwayne would do."

"That's for sure. But he isn't around...I hope."

We got on our bikes and searched for Paint. We looked for him at our hideout, in alleys and streets, and our favorite spots along the river. But we didn't find our dog.

Paint didn't show up the next day either. But on the third morning before the sun came up I heard a scratching and whining at our back door. I crawled out of the bedroom window and there stood Paint. He looked mighty poor, but he whined again and wagged his tail as I threw my arms around him.

He kept on whining. I looked him over then and was shocked when I spied dried blood and a little round hole between and above his eyes. There was more dried blood and another little hole near the back of his head. Paint had been shot. Tears began pouring from my eyes.

I crawled back through the window and put on my shoes, shirt and jeans without waking Ralph. I climbed out the window again and set out for Dr. Hammond's house, coaxing Paint to follow. I pounded on Dr. Hammond's door. When he opened it his hair was all mussed up and he was in his pajamas. He yawned and I could tell he wasn't very happy about seeing me and Paint so early in the morning.

But when I explained he took a look and said, "You're right. Someone has shot that dog. Bring him on in."

Dr. Hammond poked a needle in Paint and, when the dog was asleep, he began probing the wounds.

After a while he whistled and said, "That's downright amazing. It looks like a .22 caliber bullet hole. The slug entered between his eyes and the angle was such that it grazed along the skull and came out back here." Dr. Hammond pointed. "I don't think there's any serious injury. But the shock must have knocked him cuckoo. That's one lucky dog."

"How long will he be laid up?" I asked.

"He'll be okay as soon as he wakes up. May be a little groggy for a while. That's all."

I asked Dr. Hammond how much I owed him on top of pulling out the porcupine quills. He waved the question aside and said maybe he'd get Kenneth and me to do some work for him sometime when he needed it.

When Paint was able to stand up, I decided to take him back to Kenneth's house where the dog could recuperate in the garage. Other than not being as frisky as usual Paint seemed to be okay as we walked along. At Kenneth's house I whistled and he came outside. He grinned and then knelt and hugged our dog while I told him what had happened. Kenneth looked at the bullet holes and he started crying and cussing whoever it was that had shot old Paint.

Just then Kenneth's father came into the yard from one of his railroad runs. He stopped short and looked as if *he* had been shot. Paint stood up and growled deep in his chest and showed his teeth.

Kenneth's father said, "I thought I got rid of that damn dog. Next time I'll make sure." Then he stomped on into the house.

I looked at Kenneth. Tears were running down his cheeks.

"We gotta find someplace else to keep Paint," I said. He nodded.

It took us the rest of the day to figure it out and make the arrangements. We made a deal with Mrs. Redd to keep Paint in her old chicken coop. First she said we'd have to supply her with ten suckers a week for her cats. We bargained for a while and finally settled on six fish a week. In return she would feed our dog and keep him in her old chicken coop. It had a nice place for him to sleep and a sizable area enclosed with heavy poultry fence on the sides and over the top. Mrs. Redd said that was to keep the varmints out when she used to keep chickens.

We knew Paint wouldn't be very happy penned up like that, but we promised him we'd come by at least once a day. When we left him late that afternoon both Kenneth and I were wiping away tears as we backed away and watched Paint sitting dejectedly inside the fence.

So early every morning we would go over to Mrs. Redd's place and let Paint out and he would spend the day with us, roaming the alleys and streets, looking for bottles, fishing, and adventuring along the river.

Catching six suckers a week began requiring more and more of our time. We concluded that we had caught just about all the fish in the big hole at The Logs. So we roamed up and down the river until we found a couple of holes where the fish were more plentiful.

Chapter Eight   September

The summer vacation from school, which three months earlier had seemed to stretch endlessly ahead, all at once was nearly over. But that year we got a bonus. School was to begin almost a full week into September, the day after Labor Day.

During that week an older cousin, Walter, came to visit us. He chummed around mostly with Ralph, chasing after girls and stuff like that which high school boys liked to do.

One morning Ralph had gone to the grocery store and Walter, not having anything else to do, began talking to me.

"How'd you like to learn a new language that no one else can understand except you and a friend you teach it to?"

"I already know how to talk pig latin," I said.

"Aw, that's baby stuff," Walter said. "I'm talking about an entirely different and secret language which you and your pal could use and nobody else would understand what you were saying."

"Gee. That'd be keen, Walter. What do you call it?"

"It's called 'ive-Eng-live-ish.' Do you savvy that?"

"No. What's it mean?"

"I'm probably the only one in this town who can speak it," Walter said. "It means *English*." He poked me and laughed. Then for half an hour he explained how to do it. I spent the next two days practicing until I knew how to speak it fluently. I could hardly wait to teach Kenneth so we could talk without anyone knowing what we were saying.

As Walter got into his father's car to drive home on Friday, he said to me, "Sive-o live-ong, Kive-id!" I grinned and waved.

"What'd he say?" Ralph asked.

"Oh, he just said 'so long, Kid.'"

"How do you know?"

"It's a secret language Walter taught me."

Ralph snorted, "Kids' stuff!" and went into the house.

That afternoon Kenneth and I collected Paint at Mrs. Redd's and went to our favorite jungle along the river. On the way I told him about the secret language Walter had taught me and threw a few words at him for effect. He didn't know what I was saying, of course. So when we reached the jungle we flopped down and I began teaching him.

"It's very simple, Kenneth. It just sounds complicated until you know how. Take your name and break it down into the sounds of 'K,' 'enn' and 'eth.' After the 'K' you add 'ive', which you pronounce like 'I've.' Then you say the 'enn' and after it you add 'ive' again. Then you say 'eth' and you've got it. Kive-enn-ive-eth. That means Kenneth!

"And if a word starts with a vowel—you know what *they* are—A, E, I, O, U—then you just say 'ive' first. Like for English. You say 'ive-Eng-live-ish.' And nobody else but me will know what you say."

"Say, that's pretty keen, Johnny. But I don't know whether I can get the hang of it. You're a lot better speller than I am."

"But Kenneth, you don't know have to know how to spell a word. Just break it up into sounds and put 'ive' after each one."

We practiced the rest of the afternoon and Kenneth became nearly as good as I was. Paint got onto it right away. When I'd say, "Cive-ome hive-ere, Pive-aint," he'd come right away and look up and wag his tail, just like always.

When I entered the kitchen late that afternoon, my mother was standing at the stove poking at the coals in the firebox.

"Hive-ell-ive-o, Mive-om," I said. "Ive-I live-ove yive-ou."

"What's that you said, Johnny?"

"I just said 'Hello, Mom. I love you.'"

She smiled and shook her finger at me. "When you say that, speak English, young man. Now scoot out and get me a bucket of coal or you won't get any supper tonight."

The next Tuesday Kenneth and I enrolled in the seventh grade school on the other side of Main Street. We were assigned to different homerooms. Mine was ruled by a pinch faced old maid named Miss Shaw. Ralph had told me she was a terror and that I should pray I didn't get her. But I did. She also taught English and history.

I wished earnestly that Miss Owen was again my teacher. And when I thought of her, I'd remember Dwayne and feel that familiar terror which thinking about him always brought me. There'd been no word of him for months. I wondered where he'd gone and hoped he was dead, too.

One day in the schoolyard while I waited for the bell to announce the end of the lunch period, a strange boy came up to me and asked whether I'd like some chocolate. He held out three little pieces unlike any chocolate I'd ever seen. I popped them into my mouth. They tasted a little strange, but chocolate was chocolate. I hadn't had any candy for quite a while, not since all the suckers we caught had started going to Mrs. Redd for Paint's keep.

The strange kid walked with me toward the door when the bell rang. He wore a mean sort of grin. Just as we parted inside the school, he said, "That chocolate I gave you was

Ex-Lax. You know, the laxative. It'll make you crap in your britches if you don't watch out." Then he ran off down the hall, looking over his shoulder, grinning evilly at me.

Later that afternoon in Miss Shaw's history class I began to feel rumblings in my lower bowels. So I raised my hand as Miss Owen had taught us to do and said, "May I be excused?", catching her in mid sentence.

She glared at me and said, "Certainly not. The class period is almost over and you can go then."

I sat there a while longer and then knew I must leave or suffer eternal embarrassment. I jumped to my feet and hurried straight for the hallway door with Miss Shaw shouting "Stop. Stop! Don't you leave this room."

Miss Shaw gave me a note to take home to my mother. She read it and began scolding me for disobeying the teacher until I explained the circumstances. She gave me a hug and then said, "Well, teachers make mistakes, too, sometimes. I'll write Miss Shaw a note. And I'm sure she will forgive you this time."

I don't know whether Miss Shaw ever forgave me or not because not long afterward I got myself into another scrape which, in her eyes, was absolutely unforgivable.

Although you would never suspect Miss Shaw's being very passionate about any subject, she did have one abiding obsession which Ralph had warned me about. Miss Shaw was a zealous admirer of Sacajawea, the Indian woman who helped Lewis and Clark explore the Missouri and Columbia river basins. During four weeks of study devoted to that subject, I heard everything there was to know and much that was uncertain about Sacajawea. I heard about Sacajawea until my eyes would glaze over and I'd fall asleep. Then Miss Shaw would come down to my desk and smack me across my shoulders with her blackboard pointer.

Since Miss Shaw also taught English it was only natural that she would assign us to write compositions on Sacajawea. One day toward the end of the four-week study of Miss Shaw's favorite character, she gave such an assignment: to tell why Sacajawea was one of the greatest women who ever lived. And this is what I wrote and handed in to Miss Shaw.

> Sacajawea was an Indian woman who helped Lewis and Clark a lot when they explored the wilderness. She helped them so much that some people think she was such a great woman that they can't stop talking about her for a month. Actually there was a lot of women who were greater than Sacajawea. Such as Martha Washington and Betsy Ross and Annie Oakely and Calamity Jane and Pocahontas and my Mother.

The morning after I turned in my assignment Miss Shaw called me up to her desk and handed me a sealed envelope with my mother's name written on it. When she handed me the envelope I thought Miss Shaw looked at me more sternly than usual, but maybe not because she always looked very sternly at all her pupils.

After school that afternoon I gave the envelope to my mother. She opened it and took out two pieces of paper. One was the note from Miss Shaw. She read that first. From her expression, I gathered that the note was not complimentary and concerned me. Then she read the other paper which I could see was my composition on Sacajawea. When she finished reading it there was a little trace of a smile on her lips, but it faded fast while she fixed me with her no-nonsense look.

"Johnny, why on earth did you write such a thing as that when obviously it is her favorite subject...to spend a whole month teaching you about Sacajawea?"

"Well, Mom, I got pretty tired of hearing about the same old thing day after day. And in her English class she's always saying how the important thing is to be brave enough to put down your deepest thoughts in your own words. And that's what I did."

"There's a big difference between being brave and foolhardy...and between brave and vindictive. You were trying to get even, weren't you?"

I hung my head and mumbled, "Yeah, I guess I was. But what I wrote was what I really thought."

She laughed. "Imagine, putting your mother in the same class with Pocahontas, Calamity Jane and those others. Now your mother will be brave and meet with Miss Shaw after school tomorrow to discuss your attitude. And I want you to make sure it improves."

"Oh, it will, Mom. I promise. Besides she said yesterday we are through studying Sacajawea."

"And there's something else you should know, Johnny. You've got years of school ahead of you. If you're lucky, you may occasionally get a near perfect teacher. But most of them will not be perfect. You must learn what you can from each of them. And remember that an education is not something you are given. It's something you must *earn* by your own effort. And not everything you learn will come from a teacher or from a single textbook."

"Yes, Mom," I said. "Now can I go over to Mrs. Redd's and see Paint?"

She sighed. "I hope someday you can bring him back here. But not now. We're still eating too close to the bone. I couldn't pay all the rent again this month. I paid $12 on it, but that leaves $10 still to be paid...somehow."

Chapter Nine October

The October mornings held a hint of frost and the afternoon sunlight slanted through the reds and yellows of the leaves making the trees appear to be on fire with color. Spending hours in school rooms was painful when outside the most glorious and saddest season marched toward winter's sleep.

Kenneth and I spent many hours catching suckers for Paint's keep. But not far ahead was the freezing of the river, when we would no longer be able to fish at all.

After school one afternoon we sat on the river bank hopefully watching our lines in the water for a sign that fish were nibbling at our baits. Paint was lying nearby, snoozing in the warm October sun. Big, puffy white clouds sailed overhead in a pale blue sky.

"It won't be long 'til we can go ice skating again," I said. I pulled in my line, examined the bait, and then cast it out again into the hole.

"Yeah," Kenneth agreed, "but when the river freezes how're we gonna catch suckers to pay Mrs. Redd?"

"I been thinking a lot about that. We gotta find another way to pay her. We can't take Paint back to *your* house, and my mother says *we* can't keep him yet."

"So what're we gonna do?"

"How about trapping...and selling the furs? I just read this book by a man named Ruxton. It's called *Life in the Far West*. It tells all about mountain men catching beavers and selling their hides."

"There ain't many beavers around here."

"But there's muskrats. Lots of 'em. You know that Anderegg place near Mrs. Redd's store? His sign says 'We Buy Hides and Furs'. Maybe we could catch enough to pay Mrs. Redd all winter."

Kenneth was silent while he thought about it, then he said, "But we don't know how to catch muskrats. And where are we going to get a trap?"

"We'll *learn* how," I said. "We know where muskrats live. In those holes in the river bank. Let's ask Dr Hammond about a trap. His barn is full of old stuff. I bet he's got a trap or two in there someplace."

"It'd beat fishing all the time. Fishing ain't so much fun when you *have* to do it."

I agreed. We caught two suckers that afternoon and took them to Mrs. Redd. We had to catch four more that week to pay for Paint's keep. We left Paint looking mournfully from his pen and started for Dr. Hammond's house. When he came to the door we told him about our plan.

He said, "I trapped muskrats when I was about your age. It's a good way to earn a little money."

"Well," I said, "we're wonderin' if you might have a trap—that you would lend us—until we make enough money to pay you."

"I sold all my traps years ago. But come on out to the barn. Maybe there's one or two in all that junk."

It was getting dark inside the barn as the three of us searched through piles of this and that—carpenter tools, garden tools, coffee cans filled with bolts and nails, coils of wire, cans of paint, a stack of old furniture.

Then in a dusty corner Dr. Hammond reached behind some shovels and brooms leaning against the wall and said, "Here's one, boys." He took the trap with its dangling chain to better light near the door and examined it.

"It's pretty rusty," he said. "But that won't matter. It'll work just fine. Here, I'll show you how to set it." When he depressed the trap's spring its two jaws fell open and he placed the end of a little hinged strap across one of the jaws and into a notch on the round, flat trigger pan. Then he slowly released the spring. He took a broom handle and poked the trigger and the jaws snapped tightly shut.

"That's all there is to it," he said. "What you have to do is find a muskrat's hole in the river bank and set the trap nearby in shallow water. Sometimes it helps to hang a bait—like a carrot—over the trap. Then when Mr. Muskrat tries to take a bite, you've got him. Just keep trying and you'll get the hang of it. When you catch one, bring it by and I'll show you how to skin and stretch the hide."

"Gee, thanks, Dr. Hammond," I said, "It looks like you've put us in the fur business."

"Good luck, boys," he said.

The next day after school Kenneth, Paint, and I prowled along the river looking for muskrat holes. We found several and finally picked one and set our trap.

In bed that night it was hard to go to sleep. Just like before opening of the fishing season. My mother had okayed my plan to rise early the next morning and go with Kenneth to check our trap. But I had to promise I'd get to school on time.

I set the alarm clock for 5 o'clock. That would allow nearly four hours before I had to be at school. When the alarm went off, Ralph groaned and then cussed until I shut it off. Outside it was cold with a light breeze blowing. I was glad I'd put on my warm coat.

The sky was peppered with a zillion stars that seemed brighter than I'd ever seen them. To the south hung the constellation called Orion. Miss Owen had told us that the ancients believed it to be a sword hanging from the belt of a giant hunter. The darkness, the cold air, and the utter silence of early morning made me shiver. I thought about Dwayne and wondered where he might be and whether he would ever come back to get even with Kenneth and me.

I met Kenneth at the Logs and we walked about a mile down the river to the place where we'd set our trap. By that time there was just enough light to see our trap in the shallow water where we'd placed it. But its jaws were unsprung. We hadn't caught a muskrat. Kenneth had brought a carrot. So we cut a willow shoot, speared the carrot on one end, and stuck the other end in the river bottom to hang the carrot just a few inches over the trap.

I said, "We don't need to get up so early next time."

"No. There must be nearly three hours until school starts."

"Well, we had to allow enough time to skin our muskrat...if we caught one."

"I thought sure we'd have one," Kenneth said. "I guess there's no easy way to make money."

We caught the first muskrat Saturday morning. We took turns carrying it to Dr. Hammond's house. He showed us how to skin it without damaging the fur and he whittled an oval-shaped end on a shingle to stretch the hide with the fur on the inside and the skin out.

"That's a nice one," Dr. Hammond said. "It's a prime skin. If it weren't, you'd see black splotches on the hide, which means the muskrat wasn't fully ready for winter. And those hides aren't worth as much as a prime one like this. Now just hang it up out of the sun and in a few days it'll be dry. Then you can sell it."

"Golly, how much do you think it's worth?" I asked.

"I don't know. It's been a long time since I sold a muskrat skin. But it should bring a good price."

We checked our trap every morning without catching another muskrat. So we moved the trap to another place. On Wednesday after school Kenneth and I took our hide to Anderegg's warehouse. Inside were stacks of dried hides—deer, elk, and cattle—and a strong odor of decaying flesh. From somewhere in back old man Anderegg emerged. He was a wrinkle-skinned, sour-faced man with piercing, shifty eyes.

"I see you got a musk'at skin," he said. "Hand it over." He examined the skin, glancing at us from time to time. Then he announced, "It's got a nick in it, and it ain't prime fur. But anyways I'll give you two bits."

We gasped and looked at each other. We were expecting at least 50 cents.

I said, "Dr. Hammond skinned it himself and he said it was a prime skin."

"Does Dr. Hammond buy furs?" the old man asked slyly.

"No, but..."

"That's all I'll pay. Take it or no. It don't make me no never mind one way or t'other." He turned away and began straightening a pile of cow hides.

Kenneth and I talked it over and decided 25 cents was better than nothing. I handed the old man the skin. He fished in a pocket and tossed me a quarter.

Outside we got on our bikes and rode away. Kenneth said, "That old tightwad. I'll bet that hide was worth more than that."

"Yeah. The trouble is we don't know how much. But you know, Kenneth, I was looking through a hunting magazine in the library the other day. And I saw an ad from an outfit that buys furs in Kansas City. Let's go look up the address. We'll write 'em a letter and ask what they pay."

We used three cents from our quarter to buy a stamp and mailed the letter that same afternoon.

We caught another muskrat that week and we skinned it and stretched it ourselves. That Saturday we checked our trap and then poked along the river. Paint was ranging around all over the place, happy to be out of his pen. We heard him barking down the river a ways. I hoped he hadn't found another porcupine.

When we caught up with him, we saw he was barking at something in a pile of driftwood which had floated downstream during high water and had hung up there on the river bank. We approached cautiously and saw Paint was barking at some kind of a big furry animal in the tangle of logs and branches.

I poked the animal with a stick. It didn't move. It was dead. I grabbed one foot and pulled it out to the bank. It was heavy. Its tail was shaped like a paddle, bare of fur, large, flat, and thick-skinned. It smelled okay so it couldn't have been dead very long.

"Kenneth," I chortled, "I believe Paint's found us a *beaver.*"

"I wonder if we should skin it like a muskrat," Kenneth said.

"I think we better take it to Dr. Hammond. He'll know."

The dead beaver was nearly as big as a cocker spaniel dog but with much shorter legs. So with each of us holding one hind leg we carried the heavy animal to the doctor's place. He came to the door and said, no, he wasn't busy at the moment.

He looked at the beaver and exclaimed, "Where in the world did you get *that?*" So we told him and asked whether he'd show us how to skin it. He said he didn't have much experience skinning beavers but he would show us how the old time fur trappers had done it.

He went into his house and came back with a sharp knife. When he finished skinning the beaver he said, "See those two little holes near the head? Someone shot this animal and it must have gotten into the river and floated down to where you found it."

Dr. Hammond fashioned a round hoop by tying together two slim ash tree branches. He threaded a heavy cord through an edge of the hide. Then he ran the cord around the outside of the hoop and back through an edge of the hide an inch farther along. He continued until the hide was stretched tight and flat inside the hoop.

"Well, there it is, boys," He said. "Let it dry here in the barn for a week and then you can try to find a buyer. I don't know what a beaver skin is worth. But it should bring a good price."

A week later we took the dry beaver skin to Anderegg's warehouse, thinking he would probably cheat us but not knowing where else we could sell it.

Inside the warehouse the wily old man showed surprise when he looked at our beaver skin. He examined the skin side carefully and pointed to the bullet holes. Then he turned it over and stroked the silky brown fur.

He scratched his head and squinted up at the ceiling. "Wal," he said, "I'll give you a dollar for it."

I looked at Kenneth and saw he was astonished, too. I said, "Why, we heard a beaver skin was worth ten or fifteen dollars. Maybe more."

The old man squinted at me out of the corners of his eyes. "Do you boys have a permit for this beaver?" he asked, with a sly little smile.

"What permit?" I said.

"The law says you gotta have a permit to take a beaver. And if you don't there's a big fine and maybe jail, too. Now, I could turn you in and probably collect a reward. But we wouldn't want to do that. Would we?"

"But we didn't trap it or shoot it. We *found* it dead...along the river."

He spat on the floor. "You've got the hide. How're you gonna prove you didn't kill the beaver?" He squinted at a stack of cowhides and then back to the beaver skin. "Boys," he said, "I'll give you a dollar and a half. That's the best I'll do. If you wanna take a chance on going to jail, take it somewhere else."

We were frightened about not having a permit. So we surrendered our beaver skin and he handed us three fifty-cent coins.

Outside, Kenneth kicked angrily at the dirt and said, "That old miser has gypped us again."

I said, "We oughta hear soon from that company we wrote to. And then we'll know what our furs are worth."

"At least now we've got enough money to buy more traps. I looked in our Monkey Wards catalog last night. They sell traps for 35 cents apiece. That's 25 cents less'n our hardware store charges, and *they* pay the freight. We could buy three or four for a dollar fifty."

"Four," I said. "And a dime left over. That'd really put us in business." We mailed our order that day.

A couple days later we received an envelope from Taylor's in Kansas City. Their prices excited us. They paid from 25 cents for a small, not-prime hide up to $2.50 or even more for the largest, fully prime skins. We thought bitterly that the skin we'd sold to old man Anderegg for 25 cents might have brought $2 or even $2.50 from the Kansas City firm.

"Golly, Kenneth," I said, "Now that we'll have five traps we can get rich. We can pay Mrs. Redd for the whole winter and have money left over."

"Yeah. What'll we do with all that money? It's more than I've ever seen before."

"First we gotta catch 'em and skin 'em and stretch 'em. You know what they say. A muskrat skin on a stretcher is worth more'n a dozen in the river."

We began working more seriously than ever before. With Paint ranging nearby sniffing at every gopher hole and thicket, we scoured the river bank, searching for places to set our traps.

Every morning long before sunup I'd get up and put on my warm coat. Outside I would look up to observe Orion in the southern sky. Seeing those stars and being alone in the darkness always made me think of Miss Owen floating dead and cold in the river and of the day Dwayne tried to kill me. And I knew that I would always be afraid until they caught him before he caught me.

I would meet Kenneth at The Logs and we would set out down the river to check our traps. Every few days we would catch a muskrat and by the end of the month we had ten skins. We decided to send in just one to see whether Taylor's really paid as much as they'd said in their literature. So we mailed off not our best and biggest skin but one in the middle range of size and quality. A week later came an envelope from Taylor's. In it was a check for one dollar. We were so thrilled we boxed up the rest of our furs and shipped them off.

Chapter Ten   November

November arrived and most of the leaves had fallen. First to go were the golden yellow ash leaves, followed by the reds of the mountain dogwoods along the river. And finally the willow and cottonwood leaves turned chartreuse, then yellow, then tumbled to the ground.

The mornings grew steadily colder, mostly below freezing, warming in the afternoons. The sun tracked lower across the sky, the daylight hours becoming shorter, and the nights longer. There was no doubt. Summer was over, autumn dying, and winter was near with thin ice in the shallows near the river bank. We had to break the ice to set our traps which formed first in the slower currents near the river banks. It was cold work, but we didn't mind so long as we could catch an occasional muskrat.

Kenneth and I hoped the ice wouldn't cover the river early that year, because it would end our muskrat trapping venture. We now had ten traps and it kept us busy before and after school and on weekends: setting traps, checking them, and skinning and stretching the hides of three or four muskrats each week.

I'd read how the mountain men used the scent glands from beavers to attract others to their traps. There were little strong smelling glands on the muskrats we caught. We would rub some of that on a willow shoot and suspend it over our traps. It worked better than the carrots.

Towards the end of the month I began keeping some of the skinned muskrat carcasses in the shed, where the temperature remained cold day and night, near or below freezing. I had read that in the South natives caught and ate swamp rabbits. I decided that maybe they were really muskrats, so one day I persuaded my mother to cook a muskrat.

She dissolved some salt and baking soda in water and soaked the carcass for several hours. Then she fried it and made a little gravy with the pan drippings. No one would eat it except me. But I thought it tasted as good as chicken, although I couldn't be sure of that because it had been so long since we could afford chicken.

We were paying Mrs. Redd for Paint's keep with money instead of suckers and accumulating what seemed a fortune besides. We shipped our furs to Taylor's and received at least 75 cents for the smaller skins and $2 or a little more for the largest and best quality ones. We never sold one for the "$2.50 or even more" advertised in Taylor's circular. We wondered what kind of muskrat skin would bring such a princely amount.

We were so successful that our catches along the river near town began diminishing. So we began venturing further upstream, riding our bikes out the river road to new territories. Eventually we were setting our traps two miles or more from town.

One night late in November the temperature plunged and the river froze from bank to bank. Next day it looked as though it was covered with a sheet of glass. Kenneth and I ventured cautiously out on the ice. It was so clear we could see rocks on the river bottom and an occasional fish.

"This'd be great for skating," I said. "Wouldn't have to clear off any snow."

"Sure. But it means we're all through trapping muskrats."

"Maybe we can trap other things. Like foxes."

"We've never seen any. Where would we catch them?"

"Well," I said, "I think they come out mostly at night. Besides we didn't know how to catch muskrats, either. Maybe we can learn."

Dr. Hammond told us there weren't many foxes around that he knew of, but he suggested we scout around up the river and look for holes that might be a fox den. He said to catch a fox we'd need larger traps. So we ordered one from Kenneth's Montgomery Wards catalog.

The new double-spring trap arrived one Friday and the next day we rode up the river road on our bikes with Paint trotting ahead. We poked around in the thickets looking for a hole which might be a fox den but had no success until we crossed the river on the ice. There we found a promising hole. From it came a distinctly animal odor, and it appeared large enough for a fox to enter. Paint was very excited and tried to go into the hole but he was too big. He could just stick his head in and whine and growl as though he could tell there was *something* in there. We set our trap nearby and covered it with dry sand and leaves to conceal it.

I could scarcely wait until the next morning when we could go out and see if we'd caught a fox. As we neared the place where we'd set our trap, the odor we had noticed the day before became markedly stronger and the closer we got the worse it smelled.

"I dunno," I said, "I hope that isn't how foxes smell."

"If it is, Johnny, I don't want to get any closer to one."

Paint loped on ahead. And then we heard him barking, growling and then yelping.

"You s'pose he's found another porcupine?" I said.

"Golly, I sure hope not."

We ran toward the noise, rounded a large clump of willows and stopped short. There was Paint alternately growling and yelping as he danced around a black and white animal about the size of a small dog. One of the animal's front feet was caught in our trap.

"*Kenneth!*" I yelled. "That's a *skunk!*"

"I *know*. I *know!* Pee-ooo. What a stink."

"We gotta get Paint out of there." I ran forward and just as I neared the skunk it gave a lurch and pulled free of the trap. It scurried into the nearby hole. Paint was shaking his head and pawing at his eyes. He smelled something awful. I sniffed at my hand and found I stank just as bad.

"Lordee. Lordee, Kenneth, what're we gonna do now? If I go home like this my mother will skin me."

"Well, to get rid of the smell in your clothes you have to bury them...for a week. I heard that somewhere."

"And I promised my mother I'd go to Sunday School today..."

Kenneth snickered. "The way you smell, they'll have to be awful forgiving to let you in there. Matter of fact I don't think *anybody* would be *that* forgiving...even in Sunday School."

We rode our bikes back to town and put Paint in Mrs. Redd's chicken coop. I was glad she didn't come out of her store to smell Paint and me.

When I walked in the back door of our house my mother was in the kitchen.

"Good," she said. "You made it home in time for Sunday School." Then she wrinkled her nose and came closer. "Good heavens," she exclaimed. "*What* is that *horrible* odor?"

"It was a skunk, Mom."

"Oh, Johnny! You'll be the death of me. What were you doing playing with a skunk?"

"It wasn't exactly *playing*, Mom. It was in our trap and Paint was after it and I tried to help Paint."

"Well, one thing is certain. You can't go to Sunday School smelling like that. Strip off your clothes and take them out to the coal shed."

Then she got me in the bathtub and scrubbed and scrubbed me all over with a brush and laundry soap until my skin was nearly raw from head to foot. That night both Ralph and Anna refused to eat at the table with me. I had to eat alone, sitting on the davenport. I slept on the kitchen floor that night. Ralph wouldn't let me come in our bedroom.

On Monday morning my mother scrubbed me again and then applied some of her rose water all over my body. She said I would have to go to school in my Sunday clothes, because she was going to burn my other ones. I told her I would buy new shoes, jeans and a shirt after school with my fur trapping money.

"What about your coat, and hat, and mittens? You can't wear them to school."

"I guess I'll have to buy them, too. The old coat was getting too small anyway." I sighed. "Well, there goes my fur money."

"What a waste," my mother exclaimed angrily, "when we scarcely have a nickel to spare."

As it happened, I didn't have to wait until after school to buy the clothes, because all around my desk the kids were leaning away from me and holding their noses.

Miss Shaw approached, wrinkled her nose, and scowled. "Johnny," she said, "you smell of skunk...and something else I can't identify. But you're disrupting my classroom and I won't *have* it. You'll go home and not come back until you smell halfway human."

She gave me a note for my mother and I departed with a chorus of giggles and titters following after me.

My exclusion from school stretched to a week before my mother decided I again smelled "halfway human," as Miss Shaw had demanded. But it wasn't much fun having the week off what with Kenneth and everyone else in school most of each day.

The next Saturday Kenneth and I rode our bikes out on the river road to pick up the trap we had left near the skunk's den in our rush to get away the week before. It had snowed the night before and a strong wind carried the white powder, drifting it across the road and into the brush along the river. We weren't sure we could find the trap, but if we didn't we'd have to wait until spring.

We left our bikes by the road side and began trudging through the drifted snow up the river. We crossed on the ice to the other bank, and approached the skunk den cautiously. Paint, who still smelled like a skunk himself, seemed to have no desire to confront that animal again and followed at our heels. Near the den we spied the trap's chain dangling down into the snow from the dogwood branch we'd secured it to when we set it. Tracks in the snow told us the skunk had returned to its hole early that morning after a night of hunting. The trap was only partly contaminated. Most of the skunk's "perfume" apparently had been distributed on Paint and me. Kenneth attached the trap's chain to a long stick and carried it on his shoulder toward the river.

Upon reaching the river bank I suggested we walk on the ice down to where we had left our bikes. It would be easier than thrashing through the snow drifted thickets on the other side. Kenneth agreed.

I walked ahead of him, head down against the cold wind blowing into me. My face felt numb from the cold wind. So I turned and walked with my back to the wind. I saw Kenneth's eyes open wide and heard him shout. But it was too late. I heard the ice crack and felt myself sinking into the river.

I had backed into a place where a fast stretch of the river's current had kept the ice from freezing over. As I sank down into the water, I turned and saw ahead of me a run of open water. The current carried me down toward the end of the open water where the ice began again. I reached it and tried to clamber up, but the ice broke under me. I tried again and again, feeling the ice break away and the current trying to pull me down and under the ice. I thought I was a goner. I tried one last time and reached my arms upon the ice. Then dimly I saw Paint. He was standing on the ice and he fastened his teeth on my coat sleeve and braced his feet against the pull of the current.

Faintly I heard Kenneth yelling and then I saw him running back from the bank with a long, thick tree branch. He placed it across the open channel upstream of me and I managed to get my other arm over the branch. With Paint tugging and Kenneth pulling on the branch I finally reached solid ice and struggled out upon it.

I lay there, too cold and exhausted to move. Then I heard Kenneth shout, "Johnny, you gotta get up from there. You'll freeze to death."

With Kenneth's help I managed to get on my feet and start for the river bank. By the time we reached an area sheltered by thick clumps of dogwood and overhung by huge cottonwood trees, my drenched coat and jeans had frozen solid, like steel armor, and I felt confused. Couldn't even think what day it was. I flopped onto the snow. I wanted only to rest.

Kenneth kept shaking me and yelling, "Johnny! Johnny! You gotta get out of those clothes. I'll find some dead wood and start a fire."

I lay on the snow and faintly heard him breaking branches. He came back and laid a pile of them before me. My mind felt numb and uncaring. It was as though I was watching a boring movie and not really involved at all. Kenneth piled up some little twigs, lit a match and tried to get them burning. They would flare up and then little gust of wind would blow out the fire. He did that several times and failed to keep the fire going. Then he reached into his back pocket and pulled out a handkerchief. He lit a match and the cloth began to burn brightly. He laid it onto the twigs and piled more twigs on top. They began burning, too, and Kenneth placed some larger branches over them.

He had a good fire going, but I only wanted to sleep. I closed my eyes. I awakened to find Kenneth poking me and screaming, "Wake up, Johnny. You gotta get out of those clothes. Here. I'll take off your boots and you can stand on my coat."

Behind Kenneth a big fire blazed, the flames roaring and reaching around, blown by little gusts of the wind which reached that sheltered place. I got to my knees and squirmed out of my rigid coat. Underneath, my shirt was icy cold but not frozen stiff like my coat. I decided to leave it on until my coat was dry. I shucked off my frozen jeans. Kenneth hung them and my coat near the fire on some dogwood branches. I got as close to the fire as I dared and gradually began to feel halfway human, as Miss Shaw had put it.

It was midafternoon before all my clothes were thawed and dried. I stayed near the fire until I began to think straight and, at last, was fully clothed again.

As we prepared to leave for town, I said with a laugh, "Do you think that trap was worth the trouble?"

Kenneth said, "You were lucky old Paint grabbed your sleeve. I thought you were a goner, for sure."

"Yeah, and I was lucky you found that branch...and built the fire."

"I had to burn up my handkerchief—the one I got last Christmas—to get the fire going."

"You can buy a new one with our fur money, Kenneth. Out of my share."

We sat on a pile of branches, watching the fire die. I said, "Do you know what I thought of? Just for a second when I was in the water? I thought of that time Dwayne threw me in the river. But that wasn't near as cold as this time."

Kenneth said, "If he'd been here he'd of pushed you under. And thrown me in after you."

I nodded and said, "I wonder where he's gone. I wonder if he'll ever come back."

Kenneth said, "I hope the next time we hear anything about him it's that he's in jail forever."

The wind had diminished to just a breeze as we rode our bikes home, having to push them through some of the snowdrifts along the way. I opened the back door and entered the kitchen. My mother was ironing one of Anna's dresses.

"Oh, I'm so glad you're home," she said. "It scares me to death when you're out along that river. And I worry that sometime you won't come home at all." She threw her arms around me and hugged me tight. Then she wrinkled up her nose and sniffed at my coat. "That smells like smoke. What have you been up to *this* time, young man?"

"It was cold. So Kenneth and me built a fire."

"Kenneth and *I*," she corrected me. I took off my coat and she asked, "How did your shirt get so wrinkled?"

I looked down. My shirt was wrinkled all right.

She said, "Take it off and I'll touch it up while the iron is hot." She sighed. "I'll be glad when you're in high school and get interested in girls and dances instead of muskrats and suckers and dogs and skunks."

Chapter Eleven   December

The snow was a foot deep. We wouldn't see the grass again for two months or more. Sometimes snow covered the ground until late March or early April. But I remembered last February when there had been a thaw and Kenneth and I had taken Miss Owen the valentine box of candy. And that made me think of all that had happened to her and to us since then.

Ahead was Christmas. I wished I would get some new ice skates or, even better, a .22 rifle. That would be great to carry when we were trapping along the river. But I didn't really expect to get either for Christmas. We were still eating too close to the bone, as my mother put it. I intended to give her a necklace I'd seen in Bentley's Jewelry store. It cost $2 and I'd use some of my fur money to buy it. I no longer wanted the BB gun. My old bicycle was about worn out. Maybe I could get a better one, if Kenneth and I caught enough muskrats in the spring when the ice went out.

In the weeks before Christmas, the days passed very slowly. The newspaper printed a little box on the front page with a picture of Santa Claus and the number of days until Christmas. Kenneth would tear it out and show it to me.

We made a pact. I would give *him* a present which *I'd* like to get and he would give *me* something *he* would like to receive. Then after Christmas I would trade him his gift for mine. We decided that was a good way to avoid wasting money on something the other didn't especially want.

There were only ten days until Christmas when the letter from my father arrived. As I entered the kitchen after school

I could tell right away that something exciting had happened. I could see it in my mother's eyes and in the smile on her lips, a different smile than her usual greeting. She didn't keep me in suspense.

"We received a letter from your father today—and guess what?" she chortled. Without waiting for me to guess, she told me her news. "He's coming home for Christmas. He'll be here a week from today—and stay until after New Year's."

"Gosh, Mom, that's really keen." I felt as if she'd told me Christmas had been moved up a week. I ran to her and threw my arms around her waist. She held me and stroked my hair.

"And he said in his letter he has a surprise for us," she said. "I wonder what it is. Maybe he sold a light plant—or even two. Wouldn't that be wonderful? We could..." She gave me another hug and I thought I could imagine what she was thinking—about having enough money to pay the bills and some left over.

"Just having him come home is a good enough surprise for me," I said.

"Of course. Of course. It'll be wonderful having him with us again. It's been such a long time." She sighed and let me go.

The days dragged by as they always did before Christmas but in addition to *that* was the added anticipation of my father's coming home. Ralph, Anna and I cleaned every corner of the little house with an unusual minimum of arguing about who was doing the most work.

We were all seated in the kitchen eating the evening meal the day before my father was to arrive. I had coaxed my mother to cook one of the muskrat carcasses kept frozen outside in the shed.

My mother held up a finger and cocked her head. "Hush," she said, "I think I heard a car stop outside. Oh—maybe he's come a day early."

We listened and heard a door slam shut. We all rushed to the front door and outside onto the porch. Ralph ran out to the car with the rest of us following. My mother ran to my father's outstretched arms and they hugged and kissed each other. He bent over and kissed Anna and held out his hand for Ralph and me to shake. Then he lifted his suitcase from the trunk. Ralph insisted on carrying it to the house. But Dad stayed behind and opened up a rear car door. I could see packages stacked on the rear seat. Dad took several of them and started to the house. My mother followed with the rest of the packages. It was like seeing a real Santa Claus arrive—but in a car instead of a sleigh.

Inside the house, Dad sniffed and then said, "I smell something good. Got any left for a traveling man?" He walked into the kitchen and I saw him looking at my plate. "What's that?" he asked.

"We're having stew," my mother said. "But that's some muskrat I cooked for Johnny."

My father stopped and stared back at us. "I'm not sitting at any table where someone is eating a rat," he said fiercely. "Good God, Cathy. Are things that bad?"

She laughed. "We are not eating high on the hog. But no—things are not *that* bad. It's just that Johnny likes to eat what he catches."

Anna said, "I won't eat it. I think it's nasty."

I turned and looked at Ralph. He had that amused smile on his face. Then I said to my father, "It's not really a rat, Dad. It's a MUSK-rat. They live in the water and eat bark and roots. They eat better than a chicken. A chicken will eat anything—

even peck at manure. But muskrats are nice and clean. Folks down south eat 'em. They call 'em swamp rabbits."

"And where did you get that bit of misinformation?" Dad asked.

"I read it in a book. There was a picture. It didn't look exactly like a muskrat but they both live around water. You ought to try some. It's really tasty."

My father shuddered and shook his head. "I think I'll just have a bowl of stew and some bread. And I'll eat out in the other room while you finish your rat."

It was the best Christmas season ever, even though I no longer believed in a real Santa Claus. Ralph had told me the secret four years before. At first I'd hated him for that, because I thought it'd mean there'd be no more gifts from Santa if I didn't believe in him.

But when Christmas had come that year there was a gift under the tree from Santa—a pair of leather lace-up boots with a pocket knife in a little scabbard on the side of one of the boots. And on Christmas morning I had found my stocking filled with an orange, hard candies and nuts, and a small toy, just as it was before Ralph told me the secret.

I always wondered where the gifts materialized from in those hard times—where they were hidden until they appeared as if by magic on Christmas—and where my mother and father got the money to buy them when there was so little money to buy anything.

Ralph and I had agreed not to tell Anna about Santa Claus until she was a little older, but from questions she'd been asking we knew that some of the kids at school had already been spilling the beans.

The afternoon after Dad arrived I came down with an earache. My mother heated some castor oil in a spoon and poured it into the aching ear. Then she laid a blanket on the floor behind the space heater in the dining room and told to me to lie with my ear against the warm wall in back of the heater. I stayed there, hoping that the ache would be gone before Christmas—and fell asleep.

I don't know how long it was until I wakened. My ear felt a little better but I remained where I was with the hurting ear against the warm wall. I heard voices—my mother and father seated at the dining room table.

"Is he going to be all right?" I heard my father ask.

"Yes. He has earaches every now and then. Heat and the warm castor oil seem to make them go away."

"Shouldn't you take him to a doctor?"

"We can't afford a doctor. But if it got really serious I'd take him anyway. You know that." She sighed.

"I know you would, Cathy. You take such good care of them. I wish I could send you more money."

"Speaking of that," I heard my mother say, "where did you get the money for all those gifts? I know it doesn't grow on lilac bushes or we'd be rich."

"I've been meaning to tell you, Cathy." There was a long silence then he said, "I sold the land—and the sheep, too."

"You sold our homestead land?" she wailed. "All hundred and sixty acres? And the sheep, too?" She began to cry. "We worked so hard to get that land—and now it's gone?"

"What else could I do, Cathy? I've sold only two light plants since I went to South Dakota. And I've sent you every cent I could spare from paying for my travel and keep."

"How much did you get?"

"I got a dollar an acre for the land—and 50 cents a head for the sheep."

"Oh—oh—oh," she wailed again. "That's practically—giving them away. Couldn't you at least have got—a fair price?"

"Anything you can get for something you have to sell is a fair price these days," my father said, and there was bitterness in his voice.

"All I can think of is how hard we worked to prove up on that land—building and living in that shack—hauling water from the river—the cold and the heat and the dust—and the rattlesnakes. I was so afraid of them." I heard her sobbing quietly, then she said, "I hope you kept the mineral rights. There might be oil or coal under that land. You did keep them, didn't you?"

"I didn't even think of it. When I got a cash offer, I just sold it all." They were both silent for a while. "Besides, Cathy, there isn't any oil within 200 miles of that land. And coal that far from a town—if there is any coal—is worthless."

They were silent again, for quite a spell. Then my father said, "Let's not talk about it any more. We've got a little money at last. And we're going to have a fine Christmas. This damn depression can't last forever. I think next year will be better."

"That's easy for you to say," my mother said. "You don't have to live in this dump of a house—pinching pennies—being seven months behind on the rent—and only able to pay part of it each month. I wonder how long it will be until they evict us. And then what will we do?"

"I pinch pennies too, Cathy. I hope you don't think I'm living like a movie star. I stay in the cheapest rooms. I eat a five-cent bowl of oatmeal for breakfast. A slice of bread and baloney for lunch. And for supper—crackers or bread and a few sardines. I keep dreading that I'll blow a tire. Or the car will break down."

It sounded as though he patted her hands. He said, "They won't evict you, Cathy. We've got a reputation in this town. They know they'll get every cent we owe just as soon as we can manage it. Besides who could they get to pay the rent?

Nobody who would rent this house has any money either. But I know things are going to get better. And meanwhile we are going to have a wonderful Christmas and act like we have a little money to spend for the first time in more than a year."

"Hush," I heard my mother hiss. "He'll wake up and hear us. I try not to burden them with things like this."

"Ralph and Johnny know," my Dad said. "And Anna will soon be old enough to notice she doesn't have what other little girls have."

"The other kids haven't very much either. Even those whose fathers have steady jobs. Ralph walks all the way across town to that big store where groceries are a few pennies cheaper—to help out. I used to give him a nickel when he went over there. Lately I haven't paid him. But he goes anyway. He's in high school and he ought to have a little money in his pocket and more than one pair of slacks and two shirts." She sobbed.

"...and Johnny scours the town for bottles and burlap sacks to sell. He spends most of that on candy, but he never asks me for money. And now he's been catching muskrats. I think he must have several dollars squirreled away. I've been thinking of asking him for a loan." She giggled. "He bought his own clothes to replace the ones that got skunk smell on them. I wrote you about that. And I did borrow from his birthday money when the boys broke Mrs. Klein's window."

There followed a long silence. I felt like crying so I buried my face in the blanket. Then I heard the sound of their chairs pushing back from the table and they went into the kitchen.

On Christmas Eve we all went to church. I always liked the service on that night. It was mostly singing the familiar old Christmas carols—Mrs. Bates banging out the tunes on the piano—"We Three Kings" sung by a male quartet. During a very short sermon I found myself thinking, as I always did, about the time the preacher had broken all those dishes during the meetings on the Ten Commandments—and wishing my mother had the dishes instead. Then at the end all the kids went up to the front of the church and each received a small red gauze stocking filled with hard candies—in all sorts of colors and flavors. Then we went home and had potato soup. That night I lay in the bed I shared with Ralph—being very careful not to touch him or move into any part of his half of the bed. It seemed as though I would never get to sleep. I was wide awake, eyes open, wondering what was in the boxes my father had brought with him.

"Be quiet," Ralph said. "I can hear you blinking."

"Well, I can't sleep. I keep thinking about what's in those packages. What do you guess is in 'em?"

"How would I know? If you don't go to sleep you'll never find out."

It seemed like only a moment later that I woke up. It was still dark. I nudged Ralph and said, "Do you think it's morning yet?"

"Let's get up and see," Ralph said sleepily.

We put on our socks to keep our feet off the cold floor. The clock in the kitchen said fifteen minutes after six. We went into the room where Anna was still asleep on the davenport which pulled out into a bed.

Ralph and I turned on the tree lights. Beneath the tree were the mysterious packages which had not been there the night before when we went to bed. Anna wakened and soon joined us.

"Oo-oo-ooh," she exclaimed. "Look at this big doll. I bet Santa left it for me. He wouldn't leave it for boys, would he?"

We assured her Santa most certainly would not leave either of us a doll so it must be for her. She cradled it in her arms and said, "Ooh, look. There's a fuzzy little bear. I bet Santa left that for Mary."

Beneath the tree were two long, flat, slim boxes. One had Ralph's name on it and the other had mine.

"You open yours first," Ralph said.

I slipped off the red string and opened the box. Then I froze, scarcely able to believe my eyes. In the box was a rifle. I carefully lifted it out, as though it were made of glass, so astonished was I.

Ralph hurriedly opened his box. Inside was another rifle, exactly like mine. He inspected his and then gave a low whistle. "It's a .22 Remington, just like the one down at the hardware store. Golly—I've always wanted a rifle."

"Me, too," I said. "My *own* rifle. Maybe I can shoot a rabbit. Rabbit's as good as chicken, they say."

I heard a voice behind us. "Well, I see old Santa Claus found our house this year." Dad leaned over us and picked up a box and handed it to my mother. She opened it. Inside was a new dress. Dad said, "I had a talk with Santa and he said if the dress suits you, you have to throw away that old rag you've had so long."

She threw her arms around him and kissed him. "You tell Santa that we don't throw away anything that can be used. But I promise not to wear the old one when you're around."

After the gifts were opened we had pancakes with chokecherry syrup for breakfast. And then my mother stuffed and baked a turkey. Last year we couldn't afford a turkey for Christmas dinner and so we had elk meat my mother had canned that fall. It was good but I knew turkey would be a lot better.

Dad played the stomach measuring game with us. Before we sat down to eat he used my mother's tape measure and wrote down each of our girths, including his own. Then after dinner whoever had expanded the most in inches would be the winner.

That Christmas day I ate and ate and ate—a whole turkey drumstick, dressing, mashed potatoes and gravy, candied yams, green beans with mushroom sauce, cranberries, and two pieces of mincemeat pie with whipped cream. When I finished I was so stuffed I could scarcely move. I was certain that this time I had won.

But when the measurements were taken after dinner Dad was the winner again. I was second. Dad laughed and said it was because when he was growing up he sat at dinner table between two older brothers. They always kept poking him with their elbows and this compacted the food he ate. Consequently he had been able to cram more food into his stomach and still could. He laughed again.

The days sped by. Dad took Ralph and me outside of town and instructed us in the proper handling of our rifles. He said I wasn't to take my rifle out of the house unless he or Ralph was with me. And we were never to go out shooting with more than one person.

"Why is that?" I asked.

"To prevent an accident," he said. "You can keep track of one person's whereabouts. But more than one is inviting trouble. It's asking for someone to get shot."

Every day I took Paint over to show my father. And I showed him three hides from muskrats Kenneth and I had trapped. I said I was saving to buy another bicycle because the old one was about worn out. I told him that Dwayne was still on the loose and how scared I was that he would come back to town to get me and Kenneth. Dad said he thought Dwayne would lay low in some city where no one knew him.

Then, much faster than it had arrived, the holiday season was over, my father had gone back to South Dakota and Kenneth and I were back in school.

Chapter Twelve   January

One morning as we walked to school, Kenneth was very quiet. He seemed worried about something.

"Did yuh hear about Dwayne?" he asked.

"No. What about him?"

"Well, there was a story in the paper last night. They said Dwayne had been caught and put in jail down in Cheyenne."

"Good," I said. "That'll take care of him. Now he'll go to prison for a long time. Maybe they'll even hang him."

"Do you think he was coming back to get us?"

"Naw," I said with a show of confidence I didn't really feel. "Anyway, now they've got him there's nothing to worry about."

"But that ain't all," Kenneth said, looking more worried than before. "They said he escaped."

Now *I* was worried.

"I'm scared he'll come here," Kenneth said.

"Well, now he's been arrested again I'd think he'd want to get as far away as possible." I spoke calmly but my thoughts were churning. "What we've gotta do, Kenneth...is just be careful. Always stick together and not run around alone. Then if he catches one of us the other can go for help."

"Yeah. I guess that's what we better do until they catch him again."

The school bell rang and we went inside. All that day I felt again that familiar knot of fear inside me, thinking of the time Dwayne chased me and tried to kill me. But as the days passed the fear diminished and I began to believe I'd been right in thinking that Dwayne had gone far away. I thought the best news I could receive would be that they had caught him again and locked him up for good.

Late one cloudy afternoon, Kenneth and I approached Mrs. Redd's place. What with the clouds and the time of year, darkness was near, but we had to make our daily visit to old Paint.

"I tell you what let's do," I said to Kenneth. "Let's play a trick on Paint. I'll sneak in the barn and hide. Then you go and get Paint and he'll wonder where I am. You bring him to the barn and see if he can find me."

"Good idea," Kenneth said and ran off toward the chicken coop.

I entered the barn, groped to find the switch, and turned on the small bulb near the doorway. Except for 15 feet or so around the light the rest of the barn was dark. Mrs. Redd had said that's all the light she needed and it saved money. It was kinda spooky in there, but I knew Kenneth and Paint would soon come.

I turned to seek a hiding place, and just as I left the circle of light I felt myself seized by two big hands, one over my mouth, the other on the back of my neck. I was shoved forward into the edge of the light.

"Where's your pal?" a voice behind me said. The minute I heard the voice I knew who it was. Dwayne Tyler! Oh, my God, he's got me, I thought. I felt faint, terrified at what I knew was coming.

"I been watching you little bastards," the voice said. "You always come together. But I'll get him later. You go first."

I opened my jaws and bit the hand over my mouth with all my might. I heard him curse and then with his other fist he struck me over my right ear. The blow set off a lightning flash in my head—and the dim light in Mrs. Redd's barn grew dimmer—and all the strength poured out of me. Dwayne dropped me to the ground and then knelt beside me while I lay as if I were dead. I heard the barn door open, then I heard Dwayne rise to his feet.

I heard Kenneth laughing, Paint barking, then snarling, then a dull thump. I opened my eyes and saw Paint lying on the ground, stunned or dead, I couldn't tell which. Dwayne dropped a shovel and grabbed Kenneth by the throat and pulled him into the gloom at the edge of the light circle.

I struggled to my feet and ran and leaped onto Dwayne's back, clawing at his eyes. He cursed, dropped Kenneth, then reached back, tore me from his shoulders and threw me onto the floor. He raised his foot to kick me in the head. I saw Paint getting unsteadily to his feet. Then the big white dog snarled and leapt forward and ripped and tore at Dwayne's legs. Dwayne went down with the dog on top of him. Dwayne tried to fight away the dog's teeth with his hands and they became bloody. All the while Paint was growling and snarling and Dwayne was yelling, "Get him away from me."

The barn door opened and Mrs. Redd came in with her shotgun. "What's all this ruckus?" she shouted. Then she saw Paint slashing and tearing at Dwayne, who had his hands over his face.

"Oh, lordee!" she shrieked, "That dog's gone mad. He's killin' one of my gentlemen lodgers."

She raised the shotgun not ten feet away from Paint.

I screamed, "Don't shoot, Mrs. Redd. He's not..."

The boom of the shotgun blast inside the barn almost broke my eardrums and made me dizzy with shock. The impact of the shot charge blasted Paint from Dwayne's body and onto the floor.

I shouted at Mrs. Redd, "That ain't one of your lodgers. That's Dwayne Tyler. The one who murdered Miss Owen... and tried to kill me and Kenneth."

Mrs. Redd stared at me, mouth open, her eyes showing astonishment and confusion. She bent over and peered at Dwayne, who was clutching a terrible wound on one leg with bloody hands, blood pouring from a gash on his face. He tried to rise and fell back.

"Lord in heaven, you're right," Mrs. Redd mumbled. "He *ain't* one of my gentlemen lodgers. You say he's Dwayne Tyler...that killed Miss Owen?"

I nodded. Kenneth had gotten to his feet and came over and stared at Dwayne and Paint's body nearby. Then he started crying.

Mrs. Redd said, "Kenneth, you go in the store and phone the police. I'll see he doesn't get away."

I crawled over and took Paint's head in my lap. Blood was pouring from a big hole in his side. I stroked his fur. He opened his eyes and then licked my hand. Slowly his eyes glazed over and then his eyelids closed. He stopped breathing. He was dead.

Epilogue

That winter snow had covered the ground since the first storm before Thanksgiving and fell periodically, throughout January, February and March. It fell and compacted. And on the roof of our house the heavy snow was 3 feet deep—and deeper in places where it had been drifted by the winds. Ralph and I climbed up a ladder onto our roof and shoveled and pushed the snow off to the ground because my mother feared the snow would cave the roof in. And all over town some roofs did collapse under the weight of the snow.

There was fine skating on the river ice that winter. But it was a constant chore, shared by the neighborhood kids, to keep the snow shoveled off of the area where we skated and burned old car tires for warmth. It was late in March when the snow finally melted to reveal brown lawns and fields and announce the promise of spring.

All that time the frozen body of our dog Paint had remained in Mrs. Redd's old chicken coop shed, waiting for the ground to thaw so Kenneth and I could bury him. Dwayne was safely behind bars in the state prison. But I had frequent nightmares in which I would feel Dwayne strike me—and see him choking Kenneth—and Paint attacking him—and Mrs. Redd blasting that big hole in Paint's side. I would wake up screaming, and Ralph wouldn't get angry. He would talk gently to me, saying, "It's okay, Johnny; don't be afraid," until I'd fall asleep again.

So I was glad that first Saturday in April when the ground had thawed enough to dig a grave for Paint. Kenneth and I borrowed Davy Kilbourne's big coaster wagon. And Anna begged to be allowed to go to Paint's funeral. So the three of us took the wagon over to Mrs. Redd's place. It was still cold inside the shed where Paint's body lay stiff across the chicken roosts. Kenneth took hold of the dog's head. I lifted the hind quarters. The body was still partly frozen. We carried Paint outside and placed him in the wagon bed. Anna stood by the shed door, sniffling.

Mrs. Redd came out the back door of her store and watched us as we began to pull the wagon away.

"It's a good time to bury your dog," she said. "I don't know how much longer he'd keep in that shed. When you get him buried come back to the store and we'll have a wake."

"What's that, Mrs. Redd?" I asked.

"It's what the Irish do after a funeral. It helps to get over the pain of it. I'll give you each a bottle of soda pop and some cookies. And then you'll feel better."

We started north toward the river bottoms. We knew the place where we'd bury our dog—a small clearing amongst the tall cottonwood and boxelder trees that we called our jungle—where we'd often played with Paint at Tarzan, and Robin Hood.

First Kenneth and then I would pull the wagon while the other carried the shovel. Anna trudged along behind, singing over and over again the only song she knew. "Onerd christin so-oh-oh ohjers—Marshin ah-ahn to wah—With the cross of Jee-zus—goh-in on bee-foh."

We found the path that led into our jungle and pulled the wagon along. From above in the trees and all around from the willows and alder bushes a choir of birdsongs accompanied our somber parade—sweet trills of warblers and finches and the shrill cries of blackbirds. And Anna sang her song.

The sun's rays were almost hot and the ground was soft in the clearing where we stopped. We perspired as we took turns digging in the soft earth. When the grave was dug we lifted Paint from the wagon, folded his legs, and laid him on his side in the ground. Then we filled in the grave. I looked at Kenneth and saw tears running down his cheeks. My eyes were wet, too. Anna sobbed quietly, singing no more. But from above and all around us came the music of the birds.

With my pocketknife I cut a long and a short piece of willow shoot and tied it into a cross with some string from my pocket. I pushed the cross into the ground above where Paint's head would be.

"Somebody's gotta say a prayer," Kenneth said. "But I don't know one."

"I don't either," I said, "but I'll say something." I thought for a minute and then said what I hoped was a prayer.

"Dear God—Paint was a good dog and we loved him and will miss him something fierce. If there are dogs in Heaven we hope you'll let him in—'cause he never hurt anybody—except Dwayne—and *he* had it coming to him. Amen."

We started back down the path, pulling the wagon. I looked back at the mound of dirt and the cross. I felt tears flowing from my eyes.

"Goodbye, Old Paint—I'm gonna miss you," I sobbed. Then I said it one last time. "Goodbye, Old Paint."

Made in the USA
San Bernardino, CA
17 March 2013